MAGICKAL TROUBLE

Warlocks MacGregor®

MICHELLE M. PILLOW

MichellePillow.com

About Magickal Trouble

Magic, Mischief and Kilts!

A modern-day Scottish paranormal romance by NYT Bestselling Author Michelle M. Pillow.

When warlocks play matchmaker, things are bound to go wrong.

Warlock Bruce MacGregor likes his life exactly the way it is. He has his art, his books, his freedom. But lately, his family has become marriage obsessed. As one of the last single men standing, they're all looking at him to find eternal happiness...and they're not above casting a few spells to ensure it happens.

Author Updates

Join the Reader Club Mailing List to stay informed about new books, sales, contests and preorders!

http://michellepillow.com/author-updates/

Note from the Author

The term "warlock" is a variation on the Old English word "waerloga" primarily used by the Scots. It meant traitor, monster, deceiver, or other variations. The MacGregors do not look at themselves as being what history has labeled their kind. To them, warlock means magick, family, and immortality. This book is not meant to be a portrayal of modern day witches or those who have such beliefs. The MacGregors are a magickal class all their own.

As with all my books, this is pure fantasy. In real life, please always practice safe sex and magic(k).

To My Readers
Thank you for cheering along with the magickal MacGregor clan and supporting their crazy antics. They couldn't do it without you!

Chapter One

Hotel Motel, Green Vallis, Wisconsin

As far as first dates went, this wasn't the worst. Yes, the half-snake, half-woman wanted to eat him, but at least she didn't spend three hours listing the faults of her ex-boyfriends. Bruce MacGregor watched the thick tail slither along the floor from his place underneath the motel bed.

Bachelorhood had worked well for centuries. He saw no reason to change things now just because every other member of his extended family had started falling in love and getting married. He wasn't looking for his *fíorghrá,* his true love. Bruce liked the idea of love, just like he enjoyed a good novel. But, at the end, the book always closed, and it was on to the next adventure.

Like all MacGregor warlocks, he had his

needs. Sexual energy gave power to magick, but there were other, less complicated ways to fuel their powers. Magick did not materialize out of nothingness, though it looked like that's what happened to outsiders. No, the energy had to come from someplace. That was why they had chosen to live surrounded by the forests of Wisconsin. They could take tiny pieces of life force from the forest as a whole without damaging a single tree.

Bruce liked to think his more animalistic, primal nature didn't control him. He lived simply. He didn't need to use much energy.

If he wanted a woman to hook up with, he didn't need his family's help finding a date. That didn't stop them from trying to play matchmaker. Well, *some* of his family played matchmaker. The others were using it as an excuse to prank him.

The snake's tail moved along the end of the bed toward the motel room window and then back again as Echidna paced. Magickally conjuring the woman out of Bruce's painting was his Uncle Raibeart's idea of a joke. Now Bruce had to lay perfectly still until the creature got tired and returned to the wall where she belonged.

Why couldn't he have painted a hot, non-committal fairy or something? Or a woman obsessed with watching demolition derbies and UFC? That could have been cool.

Though, he supposed it could be argued that Echidna was the perfect woman. Her top half wasn't bad to look at. She was badass. Self-sufficient. Handy in a magickal battle.

Bruce heard a long hiss and frowned.

And hungry.

She paced into the bathroom.

Could tails technically pace?

When Echidna didn't immediately return, Bruce pulled himself out from under the bed in the opposite direction. He rolled onto his hands and knees before pushing off the floor toward the motel room door.

The second his hand touched the metal knob, he heard a loud hiss.

When he turned, Echidna was in mid-strike. His warlock magick surged forth in defense like a blue cloud to push her back. The creature slid a few feet but quickly regained her balance.

Echidna resumed her attack, hissing angrier than before. She thrust up on her tail, nearly reaching the ceiling. Her womanly top half was naked with arms that spread wide to brandish clawed fingers. The tail started at her waist, making supple flesh morph into scales. The greenish brown of her skin mimicked her tail. She wasn't beautiful in a classical sense. Well, honestly, she wasn't beautiful in any sense unless you were into monster porn.

"Easy there, love." Bruce smiled as he tried to soothe the woman inside the creature.

Echidna was immune to his charms. She hissed louder, diving forward with outstretched hands. Her tail swung around, slapping him on the back of his knees. His legs buckled, and he flung onto his back. The air was knocked out of his lungs.

His shirt and kilt stuck to the floor when he tried to roll, gluing him down.

Echidna's jaw unhinged as if getting ready to devour him.

"Sorry, sweetheart, I have a rule." Bruce used his magick to bring the mattress between them before thrusting the creature back. "No kissing on the first date!"

A loud *splat* sounded before the mattress thudded against the wall.

Bruce peeled himself off the floor, realizing he'd slipped in wet paint. The muddy green ruined the carpet in trails where Echidna had slithered across. It caked the back of his thighs and uncomfortably plastered the kilt to his skin. He cautiously walked toward the mattress against the wall and peeked around the edge before forcing it back. The painted image of the snake woman was plastered on the wall, her mouth wide and her clawed hands outstretched. A mirrored image smudged the mattress and a section of the comforter that had not fallen completely off when he threw it.

This was not how he had painted her.

In fact, it was better.

Bruce frowned as he stared at the new painting. This begged the question, could the pursuit of art kill the artist?

"Not today, sweetling," he whispered to the creature.

Damn. He wished he had painted this new version.

His attention went to the unfinished background. The landscape was the same, except for a shadowy splotch. He leaned closer. The anomaly looked like it could have been a woman in the distance. He stroked his thumb along the head shape, causing a smear of shoulder-length dark hair.

"What are ya doing, love? It's not safe in there," he whispered, trying to lean closer as if that would bring details into focus. He felt drawn to the smudge as if he had met the imaginary woman in a dream.

"Oh, for fuck's sake, Cory," Maura exclaimed behind him.

Bruce glanced over his shoulder to the motel doorway. It was an old nickname, one he wished they'd forgotten already. So what if he had a phase in the 1980s where he dressed like the actors from a popular vampire movie? He'd been bored. Though it had gotten them to stop referring to the time he joined that farming commune.

Bruce was a searcher. He liked immersing himself in hobbies. Right now, he was painting the motel room walls to annoy his sister.

His sister glared around at the mess before her eyes went to him. She groaned, lifting her hand as if to block the view of his ass. "Ugh, pull your kilt down. No one paid to see a naked arse."

Bruce chuckled and nodded toward the parking lot beyond the door. He jerked his kilt down to hide his painted backside. "Tell that to Uncle Raibeart. It looks like he's in the middle of his nightly performance."

Their naked uncle ran past, waving a kilt over his head like a flag. "To victory, laddies!"

If an army followed him, it was invisible.

Maura sighed and leaned against the doorframe to watch the parking lot. "I really thought marriage would tame him. At least Mrs. Uncle

Raibeart keeps her clothes on in public. Maybe she'll rub off on him."

Bruce came to stand beside her, watching Raibeart dart toward the motel sign on his way to a darkened field. "Actually, I think she sometimes joins him."

Not looking at her brother, Maura asked, "You're going to clean this up so I can check the guests in, right?"

"Can't. Enchanted paint," Bruce answered. "Have to wait it out."

"That's just perfect," Maura muttered sarcastically. Headlights turned toward them. She lifted her hand and gave a small magickal wave. The motel sign's no vacancy light turned on. "Out of all the family businesses, I get assigned to run one with ya."

The car paused and then turned back around the way it came.

"Just lucky that way, I guess." Bruce grinned.

"Ya have got to stop painting murals on the walls." Maura finally looked at him. Her expression suddenly lightened, and she laughed. "Ya realize ya have enchanted paint smudged over your face."

"No, I…" Bruce reached to feel his cheek.

"Ya do now." Maura laughed harder. "By the

way, ma's expecting ya at the house. She has someone special she'd like ya to meet."

"I'm not going to that." Bruce shook his head.

"What if this is the special lady ya have been waiting your whole life for?" she teased. "Ya act like ya don't want to be married."

Bruce wished his marriage-obsessed family would leave him alone. Just because moving to Green Vallis, Wisconsin, had proven lucky for his sister, brother, cousins, and two uncles, it didn't mean he wanted to jump into the monogamy pool. Dating was fine, but a marriage took on a whole new meaning when lifespans stretched out hundreds of years.

"Tell her ya couldn't find me. Send baby Tina instead. That will distract Grandma Cait."

Maura arched a brow. "Why would I use my daughter to help ya?"

"I'll repair the room?" Bruce grinned.

"To my standards," Maura countered. "No clown themes or fat babies shooting darts or Vegas in the 60s or furry revivals."

His smile fell a little. "Ya have no sense of fun, but fine. And that furry room was awesome."

"Deal." Maura walked down the sidewalk toward the motel office.

Bruce would have fixed the room anyway. Of course, it wouldn't have been to her standards.

Maura liked the motel to look like roadside Americana. If there was one thing Bruce knew, it was that immortality was a very long time. Keeping everything the same as expected only drew out the monotony.

Bruce closed the door and looked at the mess. He liked his life the way it was. He had his art, his books, his family, his magick, and his freedom.

"And I have ya, don't I, Echidna?" He chuckled as he went back to study the new version of his painting. Tiny streaks in the paint looked like a dozen small snakes slithering into the distance. His eyes moved back to the smudge. The hair he'd smeared had dried, and the face was more of an abstract idea. He leaned closer, staring until his eyes blurred, and he could imagine a face and a story. "I'd give anything to be in there with ya right now. What spell has ya trapped in there, sweet lassie?"

Chapter Two

"You look sick."

Elodie frowned at the video call on her phone. "Gee. Thanks, Mom."

Janelle Fairweather didn't understand a lot of things in life. Raised in a jewel-encrusted aquarium that she never considered leaving, the woman surrounded herself with people and opinions that mirrored her own. A bad day was losing a bid on some beautiful object she didn't need, and a catastrophe was a missing diamond earring that would require her to fire the entire housekeeping staff—such an inconvenience.

Elodie hated living in the aquarium. She'd begun cracking the glass at age five when Janelle fired the nanny her daughter liked more than her.

"I can tell you haven't been sleeping. You

should call Darby," her mother said.

"Darby is a hairdresser," Elodie frowned, "in New York."

"Yes, and?" Janelle arched a brow. "They have injectables and hair extensions. You can get all that fixed."

"I'm not in New York. I'm in Wisconsin."

"They don't at least have decent beds in Wisconsin?" Janelle appeared distracted by something beyond her phone. The image dipped to a ridiculous painting of a man wearing a banana peel in an unfortunate location. Wait, sorry, not ridiculous. According to Janelle, that was "*fine art.*"

"Ever since that snake bit me, I think I feel something moving by my feet when I lay down." Elodie glanced over the rest stop. Early morning sunlight caressed the building and created a dusty haze over the tall grasses along the side as a mower buzzed noisily in the distance. She'd opted to sleep in her car rather than outside in a sleeping bag.

"I don't see why you didn't just get a proper hotel," her mother scolded. "It's not like we can't afford it."

Because the book I'm writing is about a woman living rough.

…maybe.

It might be about a grown-ass woman escaping her

overbearing parents.

Fuck, I don't know.

"I tried. The no vacancy sign flashed on as I was pulling into the parking lot."

"That's not funny. Real hotels don't have vacancy signs."

Elodie took a bite of her breakfast. "It was a motel."

Her mother's expression was almost worth this phone call. "What is that thing you're eating?"

"Beef jerky," Elodie answered as she took another bite.

"I raised you better than—I can't deal with your tantrum now "

The phone was handed off to her assistant, Roberto. "Hey, princess, your mother has a meeting. You'll be back for the fundraiser, yes?"

"No."

She barely got the word out before Roberto answered, "Ok, sweetie, kisses! I'll text you the info."

The pretentious jerk hung up on her. His overly friendly fakeness made her want to push him off the penthouse balcony.

Her phone dinged, and she glanced down to see Roberto had texted her, "*Arena.*"

"Which arena?" she muttered, not that it mattered.

Elodie tore off another bite of her beef jerky. The man's real name wasn't even Roberto. It was Jim. Her mother was such a cliché.

She tossed her cell phone on the passenger seat and muttered, "Thanks for checking on me, Mom. Yes, the boulder falling off that dump trunk and hitting my car was scary, but I'm all right. And, yes, my leg still hurts, but it's getting better. It *is* strange that a snake was in the sleeping bag that I keep in my car. Oh, no, don't come to the hospital to check on me. Stop. You're smothering me with your concern. I—"

Something light tickled the top of her head, and she swatted her hand while looking for a bug. Not seeing anything, she rubbed her hair. Tiny grains of sand rained onto her shirt. She glanced up, wondering where they came from.

A light *tink-tink* sounded on the windshield. The trees in the distance started to move as the wind picked up. A woman jogged into the restrooms.

Tink-tink-tink.

Elodie opened her car door and started to push outside when grains of sand bombarded her arm and cheek. She yelped in surprise and let the wind slam the door shut.

Tink-tink-tink-tink-tink-t-tink-t-tink-t-tink-t-tink...

The gusts intensified, forcing the branches to

contort and sway. Sand pelted the car and began gathering against the windows. Dust rolled over the landscape like fog, darkening the view until it became impossible to see past the hood of her car.

"What the...?" Elodie twisted in her seat. The sand surrounded her. It piled against the windows as if to bury her alive.

She grabbed her phone and tried to check online to see what was happening. It didn't pick up a signal. She tried to make a call. It didn't ring.

What did she do?

Make a run for the building?

Stay put and wait it out?

Try to drive closer to the restroom so she had a better chance of making it inside?

The sound of sand grains stopped as there became too many of them, piling thick against the windows. She turned on her wipers. They moved the sand around but didn't clear the windshield.

Elodie tugged at her neckline, pulling at her t-shirt. Her heart quickened, and her stomach clenched. She took a deep breath as panic set in. The interior of the car darkened. She held up her phone, shining the light.

"Think, Elodie." She glanced around before crawling over to the passenger seat. She pulled the t-shirt up over her mouth and nose. Rolling down the window a half inch with the intent of reaching outside to test how bad it was, she was instantly sorry as sand blasted into the interior. She quickly reversed the action.

She couldn't get out.

Or call for help.

She was trapped.

Her breath sounded abnormally loud. She drew her knees into her chest. The phone light shut off, casting her into darkness.

Surely someone would come for her. They had to know cars were trapped here. She focused on her breathing.

"This isn't happening," she whispered.

The sound of falling sand had her pulling up the flashlight app on her phone. She pointed it at the air conditioning vents. Sand poured out of them onto the floor.

Elodie shifted in the seat and pushed her feet against the vents to stop them. She shined the light around the interior. Sand began coming out of the vents on top of the dashboard. Dust from the sand began to fill the air, and she coughed as she covered her nose and mouth with her arm.

Elodie dropped her feet and placed the phone so the light shone upward. She reached behind her seat to grab a jacket. She stuffed it against the top vent.

Nothing seemed to work.

She crawled into the back seat and pulled her shirt over her mouth and nose to filter the air. Panic made it challenging to concentrate. The light darkened, and she scrambled to get her phone before it was buried. The sand had piled on the floor and now covered the front seat.

How was this happening? It's like a dump truck released itself on top of her. No dust storm could do this. Not even the Dust Bowl from the 1930s.

Sand came from under the seat. She had no choice. She needed to run.

Elodie grabbed the handle and prepared to make her escape. She pushed at the door, unable to open it as the sand weighted it down.

Sand poured over the front seats, filling up the back. Elodie slammed her shoulder against the door as hard as she could. The light flickered as her phone was devoured by the rising threat.

"Please, please, please," she begged, kicking her legs as she tried to find footing on the shifting surface. The light disappeared. She felt the pressure building against her legs.

Suddenly she fell backward. The shirt jerked off her face, and she gasped in shock, expecting to choke.

"Oh, hey, gotcha." Hands caught her under the arms.

Those hands pulled Elodie back, so her legs fell out of the car onto the pavement. The back of her heels bounced a little as she tried to wriggle to safety.

"Easy, lassie," a woman soothed in a Scottish accent. "We'll get ya an ambulance."

Elodie grasped the hand on her shoulder and held on tight. A staggered series of, "oh-oh," came out on shaky pants.

She stared at the car, expecting sand to fall from the opened door. The interior was empty.

"Where…? Where…?" She managed to struggle to her feet. Her phone rested on the seat as if nothing had happened. "Sand?"

Elodie looked around. The restrooms were gone. Instead, she stood in the parking lot of a motel. She turned to the sign.

"Hotel Motel?" she read.

"Name came with the place when we bought it," the woman explained. "The previous owner wanted to cover all his bases."

Her rescuer's short red hair framed her face. The bright green of her shirt seemed stylish, too much so for someone who ran a motel. One of the more useless benefits of being an accessory to Janelle was the ability to size people up by the quality of their clothing.

"How did…?" Elodie went to her car. A layer

of dust covered the vehicle but no grains of sand. What was happening? "I tried to stop here, but there wasn't a vacancy."

Elodie frowned in confusion. That had been three nights ago.

"No, we have room," the woman said. "Did ya want to check in?"

A dent and long scrape from the rogue boulder marred the side panel. Elodie opened the front door and looked inside. Her purse sat on the passenger seat, covered in dust.

"Yes," Elodie finally managed. She couldn't make herself get back in the car, so she pulled the keys from the ignition and grabbed her purse before slamming the door. "I'd like to check in."

"Do ya need an ambulance?"

"I was...sleeping," she lied. "Night terrors."

She used to have them as a child. It could be true.

Or she could be delusional.

"Well, let's get ya checked in then." The woman glanced over Elodie before motioning for her to follow. "Hot shower, brand new bed, make ya feel right as rain. I'm Maura MacGregor. If ya need anything, just let me know."

"Elodie Fairweather," she answered, looking down to see she, too, was covered in dirt. "Thank you, Maura."

Chapter Three

The motel room smelled of a remodel—the fresh paint and perfect carpet fibers, having never seen a guest. Elodie sat cross-legged on the bed and stared at the reflection looking back at her. She'd brushed her wet hair away from her face. The shower had been welcome, but now she kept picturing the dark muddy trails that had come off her body as she washed.

Where did the sand come from?

Where did it go?

She'd been covered in dirt, so something had to have happened. Her clothes were still lying in a filthy pile near the bathroom floor.

Had she lost time? Some trauma? Buried alive? Had she clawed her way out of a grave?

Was some supernatural karmic force trying to kill her?

The sand had felt so real.

She didn't remember driving to the motel.

Elodie tugged the leg of her plaid pajama pants up to check the bandage. The snake bite was beginning to heal. Did the doctors miss some of the poison, and this was all a hallucination?

A tear slipped over her cheek. "What is happening to me?"

No one answered.

She picked up her phone and tried calling her mother.

Roberto answered, "Now's not a good time, princess. Your mom is getting her beauty rest for tonight. I'll tell her you called."

As her mother's voice began talking to someone in the background, he hung up on her.

"I'm scared," she whispered into the phone before slowly dropping her hand beside the bed.

Elodie felt the loneliness flooding in. It started as an ache in her chest and built until tightness radiated over her heart. She desperately wanted someone to be with her.

"Call me," Elodie pleaded via voice text to her mother's phone. She sent it and waited for an answer. She didn't get one.

Elodie stared at her phone, her mind going

through the list of people she knew. Gina, her roommate from boarding school? She hadn't talked to her in a year. Carrie? Kiki? Ambyr with a Y? They had access to a private jet but were probably on some yacht in the Mediterranean with pool boys they picked up off the coast of Who-the-fuck-knows Island. There was no way they would leave the party to fly to Wisconsin.

Jonathan, her father's old partner? He'd told her to call him if she ever needed anything. Sure, she'd been seven, and it was right after her parent's divorce.

Degenerate Uncle Keith? Would he be sober enough to leave Atlantic City?

Elodie had no one. She had a bank account full of money, but she learned the hard way that the kind of friends you could buy were not the kind she wanted to be around.

Her phone dinged several times in quick succession, and she instantly checked her messages, eager for any connection. They were all from Roberto's number.

"*She can't come to the phone right now.*"

"*Evanesce.*"

"*Sorry. Busy. Ignore that.*"

"*Even so, I'll tell her.*"

"Please do," Elodie texted back. She stared at the phone, hoping there would be more, even though Roberto wasn't her biggest fan. Minutes passed, and nothing happened.

Finally, she turned on the television and pushed the volume down so that the voices were just a soft murmur of background noise. The light flashed over the bed. Next, she left the bathroom light on but shut the door so it wasn't too bright. After checking the door locks and tugging on the curtains, she crawled under the covers. The sound of someone walking past the window caused her to stare in that direction as she lay on the pillow.

"Ma, ya did not tell her to meet me here," a man protested in a Scottish accent. "Well, maybe I already have a date. Did ya think of that?"

Elodie lifted her head to continue eavesdropping.

"What do ya mean the family made a dating schedule? Ma, I'm over four hundred years old. I can find dates."

Four hundred?

That must have been an inside joke.

"I'm not wearing the formal kilt," he insisted. "No, Ma, I don't care that the ladies think it's sexy. I don't want to—"

Elodie angled her head, hoping to get a glimpse of him pacing past.

"Then stop rescheduling with her if she's so

insulted by my no-showing. I didn't set the date. I have responsibilities to—"

Elodie sat up on the bed.

"No, I don't want a copy of my dating sched —" The man gave a frustrated sigh and began talking rapidly in another language.

"Poor dude," Elodie whispered to herself.

Being set up on blind dates by a parent sucked ass. If Janelle Fairweather had her way, Elodie would be on baby number two-point-five with Thurston Braindead the Third. The man had the laugh of a hyena and the face to match. But, most importantly, he had family wealth. What was physical repulsion and self-loathing compared to billions in the bank and a pseudo-doctor on call to send your consciousness to Happy Town?

Elodie focused on the curtains as she got out of bed and went to sneak a look at Mr. Blind Date. She dug her toes into the carpet. She couldn't understand him but instead became mesmerized by the flowing melody of his tone.

Peeking through the curtains, she watched as he drew his finger over the hood of a dirty car, tracing designs in the dust. The abstract figure of a woman appeared surrounded by squiggles that reminded her of cartoon wind.

Bare feet bounced on the pavement as he shifted his weight to one side. Paint splattered his faded jeans, and a series of old holes marred the fabric of his t-shirt. She wondered if he was one of the construction workers remodeling the rooms. He had the build of a man who knew physical labor intimately. His brown hair curled, the shaggy ends giving away his need for a haircut. Even so, the Bohemian vibes were attractive.

Her parents would hate it if she brought a man like this home. That made him all the more desirable.

"I'm always nice to the ladies, Ma," the man finally said, his tone capitulating. "In fact, I have a date already tonight."

He paused, glancing around. "I'm not lying. She's standing two feet away from me, waiting, so I must go."

Elodie leaned closer to the glass and glanced up and down the sidewalk. He was alone.

"I don't know if she wants children," he sounded exasperated. "I'll be sure to freak her out by letting her know ya want twenty grandkids."

The man swiped his hand along the hood, erasing the wind and the womanly figure. Elodie felt tingling pressure along her arm and face as his hand moved. She turned toward the darkened corner in surprise but was lifted off her feet and flung through the air.

Chapter Four

Bruce heard a loud thump and stopped walking to turn toward a motel room door. "Ma, seriously, I got to let ya…"

He hung up without finishing the thought. No part of him had wanted to have a conversation about his love life with his mother. One grandkid and suddenly she had baby fever for more.

Going to the door, he knocked. Television light flickered through the seam in the curtains, but the noise wasn't loud enough to have caused the thump. "Everything all right?"

No one answered.

A strange feeling came over him, and he pressed his hand against the door. Blue magick swirled his fingertips. The door unlocked itself, and the knob turned without him touching it. He pushed the door open.

"Everyone ok in here?"

His eyes went to the empty bed and swept over the room. The air in the room felt heavy as if someone had turned up the humidity to Louisiana swampland in July level. The door hit something, and he looked down to see a woman's leg. He instantly shut the door to look behind it. A woman slumped unconscious against the wall, her limbs strewn like she'd been flung against it.

"Reveal yourself," he ordered, watching the room for signs of life. Yellow signal lights danced up from the woman to reveal her location, but other than her, the room was empty.

He lightly touched her face before reaching to support her neck as he placed her in a more comfortable position on the floor. Standing, he waved his hands over her, spreading his magick to cover her body in a blue, shimmering light.

The woman lifted from the floor as his magick encased her, and he directed her to float toward the bed. The covers rolled back to allow his magick to lay her down.

Bruce grabbed his phone and forced it to ring without him pressing the buttons.

"Is—?" his mother started to answer.

"Ma, I need ya," he interrupted. Going to the

door, he opened it to read the number. "Room seven."

He shut the door and ended the call by dropping his phone on the nightstand.

The blue glow of his magick swirling around her began to fade, and he lifted his hand to reinforce the barrier he had created. "Take it easy, beautiful. Help's coming. My ma's a healer. She'll know what to do."

Bruce stood guard over the bed, watching the woman's chest lift with breath. Her chin-length dark hair fanned over her check. Her picturesque form was like a sculpture that had come to life. There was art in her slight imperfections, which only added to her beauty.

A familiarity tugged at him, but he couldn't remember meeting her. Perhaps he'd seen her? A passing glimpse in a used bookstore? In a car stopped next to his, waiting for a red light?

No. None of that seemed right. He felt as if he'd connected to her, talked to her.

If he'd met her, he'd know her name, but his mind drew a blank.

As a warlock, living hundreds of years, he'd met many people. It wasn't reasonable that he'd remember everyone. But she couldn't be more than thirty. So, in the last ten years? Surely he could remember that far back.

Her mouth opened slowly as if she were trying to mumble something. Bruce leaned closer, but "...doctor..." was all he could make out.

"Help's coming," he tried to reassure her.

The light of his magick danced along her cheek like a caress. He lifted his hand, wanting to touch her but not daring to break the barrier keeping her safe.

"I promise nothing will happen to ya if I can help it. I'll stay right here by your side."

Bruce liked to think his words gave her comfort because she settled. He didn't make a lot of promises in his life, but he always kept them.

The motel room door blew open seconds before his mother entered, followed by his Aunt Margareta, who suddenly stopped and lingered in the doorway.

"The magickal residue is thick in this room." Margareta frowned. Unlike his mother, who dressed like she was about to attend a business meeting in the 1950s, Margareta wore modern slacks and a loose blouse. "Cait, I think your son is dating a magick hoarder."

"She's not a hoarder." Bruce frowned.

His mother arched a brow at him. "Your aunt is right. There is a lot of magickal residue in this room. Something happened in here."

"Do we need to have the sex talk?" Margareta tried to hide her teasing smirk.

Bruce's lip curled at the suggestion.

"Do I want to know what ya did to her?" his mother added.

"Ma, she's a motel guest. She fell," Bruce pointed toward the bed. "Tripped, I think. I found her on the floor."

"Is this the reason ya stood up Ullah tonight?" his mother asked, critically eyeing the woman on the bed. She hovered her hands over the magickal encasement to sense for injuries.

"I didn't stand up Ullah. I never agreed to take her out," Bruce protested. "I don't know Ullah."

"A gentleman keeps his dates." Margareta's tone scolded, but it belied the look she tried to hide on her face. "Ullah is a perfectly sweet, um, who is she again?"

"Twelfth cousin, twice removed of that darling witch we met in the Hoia Baciu Forest," his mother answered.

"Ya want me to take out the cousin of Muma Pădurii?" Bruce shook his head. He'd never met the woman, but he'd heard stories of the Romanian immortal. They were much darker versions of Hansel and Gretel, and Muma Pădurii wasn't exactly the hero of that tale.

"Twelfth cousin, twice removed," his mother corrected.

"Powerful family," Margareta added. "It would be a nice alliance."

"Only if it's love," his mother insisted.

"Don't they eat their young?" Bruce drawled.

Margareta continued to suppress a grin. "Not for centuries."

"Not that can be proven, ya mean," Bruce countered. "Ma, please, can ya…?"

He motioned to the woman.

"She looks fine to me," his mother answered.

Bruce turned to find scared eyes staring up at him from within the cocoon of his magick.

"Though, ya might have some explaining to do," Margareta added. "If ya pluck her memory, don't tell your cousins, and don't take too many. We've had bad luck with that."

"I'm not scrambling her brains," Bruce instantly denied. Her stare held his. Blue magick swirled the woman's face. "She did nothing to us. What will be, will be."

He understood the MacGregor family's need to protect their magickal secrets. Hell, he understood the entire supernatural world's needs. No one wanted to return to the horrors of witch trials and supernatural bounty hunters. That secrecy was the one thing they could all agree on.

But it shouldn't come at any cost.

No secret was worth murder or taking some-one's memories. The magick of forgetting should only be used in traumatic situations when the target's life was made the better for it. And even then...

"I agree. No erasing memories," Cait said. "After Charlotte and Helena, that magick should be locked in the vault and forgotten."

Margareta moved to stand beside the bed.

The woman's mouth moved, but they couldn't hear her through the barrier of magick.

"My name is Cait," his mother stated. "I'm here to help ya. I'm going to need ya lie still while I check your head."

His mother nodded at him to remove his magick. Bruce obeyed, waving his hands to draw the cocoon from the woman's body.

The second he released her, the woman pushed up from the bed and began swinging her arms, screaming.

"Och!" Margareta grunted in surprise as she jumped out of the woman's way.

With a point of his aunt's finger, a yellow magick flooded the room, petrifying the woman into place. Her fleeing body became a statue, caught mid-motion.

"I think her head is fine," Margareta drawled

with a small laugh. "She's got a set of lungs on her."

A knock sounded on the door, and a man yelled, "Everything all right in there, miss?"

"I'm fine!" his mother answered. "Scary movie. I'm sorry. I'll keep it down."

Bruce leaned his head against the wall to peek through the edge of the curtains to watch the guy at the door. He wore boxer shorts, a white tank undershirt, and cowboy boots.

"You sure?" the cowboy persisted.

"Yes, thank ya!" His mother pushed a wave of calm toward the door.

"All right, then. Have a good night, miss," the cowboy said.

His mother brushed off her skirt and sat on the edge of the bed. She arched a brow at him. Bruce knew that look. She wanted him to explain himself, to explain what was happening.

The only problem was… he had no answers.

Margareta's expectant look joined his mother's.

"I heard a crash. I came in to help," he said. His eyes were drawn to the woman's face, frozen in confusion as she'd tried to flee. He regretted that fear, even as he was drawn to the artistic sculpture of her beauty. It pulled at something deep inside of him. It was the same feeling he got when he became lost in his art, in the creation of something more, those moments before completion when things were finally coming together.

"Hm." His mother nodded slowly. "Then I suppose we should take her back to the house with us and wait for her to thaw so we can mitigate any damage."

Bruce thought of her waking up in the family mansion that overlooked the town, surrounded by his aunts, uncles, and numerous cousins.

"There is no reason to risk moving her. I'll wait for her to wake up." Bruce went toward the door and held it open. "I'll take care of her."

Margareta grinned at him as she walked out of the room.

"Ma?" Bruce insisted when his mother stared at him.

"Promise me ya will be careful," she insisted. "Something is off here."

"Usually is." Bruce lightly cupped her cheek. "I'll check in with ya later."

She glanced over him. "And take a shower before she wakes up. Ya look homeless."

"Aye." He nodded as he ushered his ma from the motel room and shut the door.

"Sorry about that, lassie," Bruce said to the statue. Despite the panic on her face, he knew she wasn't in distress. He'd been hit with this kind of petrification magick more times than he could count. It felt like a dreamless sleep, at least until awareness started to return, and then it became like wandering through the hazy wasteland between dreams and wakefulness.

Sitting on the bed, he grabbed the remote and turned up the volume on the television before flipping through the channels. He stopped when he found a black and white film.

"Have ya seen this one?" Bruce asked, settling back on the bed to wait out the spell. "Classic. We'll watch until commercials and then see what else is on."

Chapter Five

What kind of new hell was this?

Elodie tried to keep her breath quiet as she huddled in the dark. Snakes. Sand. Paralyzed. Now darkness?

Her hands shook as she felt the ground. It was cold and hard, like a cave floor. Beneath her touch, it softened into carpet.

Lights flickered to reveal an unfamiliar room devoid of color. She kneeled on the floor next to a bed. The gray tones seemed a dreary choice of décor. She slowly pushed up to look over the cotton comforter. Eyes met hers, and she recoiled in fear before realizing it was her grayed reflection.

Elodie touched her face before looking at her

hands. Like the room, her gray-toned skin was devoid of her actual color.

Colorblind?

She rubbed her eyes and looked again.

Someone had turned her life into a black-and-white movie.

None of it felt right. She pushed against the carpet, trying to stand. A loud, popping groan came from outside like a tree screaming in agony before snapping in half under a high wind. She instantly dropped back down to hide. The air around her inside the room stayed eerily still.

A shriek sounded, the chilling cry of fear coming from somewhere in the house.

She wasn't alone.

It wasn't comforting.

Elodie crawled toward a window and pushed the floral curtains aside to look out at the lawn from a second-story window. The dark country-side stretched as far as she could see until it became a blur of nightscape—a dirt road cut through a manicured lawn and then the taller grasses of a field. At first, she thought the scat-tered shadows were trees...until they stumbled forward like drunks searching for the next stop in a bar hop.

"Why is this familiar?" she whispered, staring at one of the closest figures.

Light crawled over the lawn as clouds unveiled the moon. The lower half of the man's face was missing. Elodie's breath caught, and she covered her mouth to try and stop sounds from passing her lips.

Zombies! Fuck.

She dropped from sight and pressed into the wall.

Wait. Zombies?

Elodie forced herself to look again, even as a light gurgling moan came through the glass. She stared outside. A woman ran up the path, screaming as she dodged the cumbersome undead creatures.

"No, no, no," Elodie whispered, flinching as the woman got too close to the zombies. She began to stand, unsure how to help. She felt her pocket for her cellphone but realized she wore her pajamas. Who would she call anyway? Her mother, who rarely answered? The unhelpful Roberto, guardian of her mother's fake "beauty rest"? Unless Janelle was the most tired woman in the world and needed her various gym instructors to read her bedtime stories, little rest was happening.

Think.

She should have been in the motel, under the covers.

"Wake up, Elodie," she mouthed as no sound came out. She pinched and scratched her arm hard, feeling the painful sensations.

A loud thud came from below, and she dropped back to the floor. The woman's screams became louder as she begged for help.

Elodie wanted to crawl under the bed to hide. She wanted all of this to go away. Instead, she forced herself to stand. She couldn't leave the woman outside.

What if the house was locked?

What if this was some kind of cosmic test of survival?

Or a test of bravery?

Elodie forced one foot in front of the other.

"You have to shoot zombies in the head," she whispered, trying to bring forth a plan of action. "That's what all the movies say."

"Please!" the woman outside pleaded.

"You need a gun to shoot things." Elodie stumbled in her fear but continued out into the hall toward the stairs. The old farmhouse boards creaked beneath her steps.

"Did you hear that?" a man's voice traveled up the stairs.

Elodie leaned against the rail and tried to see down.

"She's leading them right to us," a woman panicked.

"I think someone's upstairs," the man said.

"We checked that already," a second man answered. "Help me open the door."

"You can't!" the woman cried. "Please, Joe, no!"

An argument followed the sounds of a struggle.

"Get off me, Linda!"

"Joe, you can't open the door. She's leading them right to us," Linda insisted. "Frank, please, tell him."

Elodie inched down the stairs. The people below sounded scared, but at least they didn't zombie gurgle. Maybe they could tell her what was going on. Or where this place was.

"Did you secure the windows upstairs?" Frank ignored Linda. "Can these bastards climb?"

"I think that's Earl," Linda said. "From up the road. Look, Joe."

"Damn it, Linda! Get away from the window," Joe ordered.

A creak sounded as a door opened. The men shouted for the woman on the lawn to hurry.

"Run!"

"Move it, lady!"

Elodie somehow managed to make it down

the stairs to better see what was happening. Two men stood at the door, yelling and waving the woman to safety. Their combination of slacks and cotton shirts rolled at the sleeves looked like Hollywood's idea of 1950s farmers. Windows had been boarded shut with broken pieces of furniture. Linda tried peeking through the cracks. Like the men, she wore period clothing.

"She's not going to make it. She's not going to make it," Linda repeated like a hysterical mantra.

"They're inside!"

Elodie gasped in surprise as she turned her attention back to Frank in time to see a fist coming for her. The hard crack shot pain through her cheek, reverberating through her skull. She tried to lift her arms, but her body didn't seem to work. A second blow followed the first, and she fell back onto the stairs.

"From salad to breadsticks, we have the extras you crave."

Elodie flailed and tried to stand. Her knees hit the bottom of a table, and she recoiled into the soft cushions of a restaurant booth. Confused, she tried to get her bearings.

Seeing movement, Elodie glanced up to find a smiling waitress in full color. The woman's mouth moved like she was having an animated conversation, but no sound came out. Elodie glanced around, seeing tables of happy families in similar situations—all having silent conversations as background music pumped from speakers.

In the center of the action was the lone voice of the manager, smiling toward windows and talking to no one. "So what are you waiting for? Join the party at Santa Fe Pizza Palace. When you're here—"

"You're family!" Everyone else in the restaurant yelled, turning toward the windows.

Elodie flinched and burrowed down into the seat. She closed her eyes, lightly touching her sore face where the man had punched her. The pain was genuine.

When she again looked, her surroundings had changed, and she found herself hiding in the back seat of a sedan. She lifted up to see a man dressed as a cowboy having a conversation with someone in a gorilla costume. They talked toward the nearby street as if performing before turning toward a car with a monkey at the steering wheel and laughing.

Elodie caught her reflection in the window and moved to look between the front seats at the rearview mirror. Red marks marred her eye and cheek. She lightly touched where Frank had hit her.

"At Wellton Motors, we don't monkey

around!" The cowboy passed by her window. "Isn't that right, Harry?"

"Oo-oo," the gorilla answered as the cowboy gave an over-the-top fake laugh.

Black and white zombies at a farmhouse. Pizza. Car commercial?

Was she inside a television?

The temperature dropped, and her body slipped. Several blurs came whizzing past. When she tried to push up, her hands and knees slipped on ice. Hockey sticks clacked on the ring as athletes chased a puck. Deafening cheers sounded, followed by booing. Elodie tried to push herself toward the side of the rink. She managed to slide into a wall, where she drew her legs up into the fetal position.

"It looks like someone got a little too excited by the action," an announcer declared. "We have a sports fan on the rink! I expect the ref will stop the play any moment now."

A whistle blew. Hockey players zoomed past.

The athletes turned into two lions brawling as they kicked up dust. Thankfully it didn't last long, and Elodie found herself once again in a bedroom. Unlike the black and white farmhouse, a large fireplace cast an orange glow over stone walls and floor. Though clearly decorated in a blend of the Medieval and Renaissance periods, the room felt more like a museum piece than reality.

She heard footsteps and looked around the display before crawling inside a trunk to hide. The cramped quarters didn't allow the lid to close all the way, and she used the small seam to watch as a man in a tweed jacket entered the room. He spoke in a heavy English accent to no one in particular about the historical significance of the castle's nobles.

"Though we know better today, during this period the fear of the unknown often led to claims of the supernatural, which were signs of the devil's work. Lord MacGregor was rumored not to age because his youthful appearance lasted way into his fifties. Instead of attributing this to good genetics like we would today, his subjects whispered about a pact with the devil. Not unlike the stories surrounding Hungarian Countess Elizabeth Bathory, whom they said bathed in the blood of young serving women to maintain her youthful…"

"…APPEARANCE, Lord MacGregor was thought to have allowed his body to be used for unearthly possession and in return was granted the powers of youth."

Bruce glanced up from his sketchpad and frowned at the television. "Och, now. Comparing us to the serial killer Countess is unfounded. We've been many things over the centuries, but never that."

He waved his hand at the television and muted the volume.

"Enough of that fool," he said to the woman's statue. "Uncle Raibeart brought those rumors on himself. He fell into a pig pen on one of his naked runs, and villagers saw him streaking, covered in muck, and smelling of filth. I'll be having a word with the museum about allowing this."

The woman didn't answer him.

"And that wasn't even Uncle Raibeart's room," Bruce grumbled, more than slightly annoyed by the inaccurate history lesson of the program.

His family still owned the property, more or less, and had the manor and the surrounding land preserved. The thought had been that one day they would move back. Royal watching had always been a human pastime, but none of them could have predicted the advancements of modern technology. Nowadays, people would pay close attention if the noble family of MacGregors moved back into a medieval castle museum owned by "ancestors". Paparazzi would camp on the lawn, and they wouldn't get a moment's peace as their lives were cast out over the internet.

"It's funny, the changes that flow through life." He doodled on the sketchbook, glancing from the television to the statue and then back to his sketch. "Even with all our magick, back then, in that castle, we couldn't have imagined what the world would become. We thought it would be simple to move back home."

If he thought about it, Bruce was sure he could name things he missed about the past, but he wasn't one to dwell in longing. If he wanted a simple life, he'd turn off his cellphone and grab a book. If he wanted adventure, he'd hike into the mountains. He'd find a werewolf biker bar if he wanted a good fistfight.

"I am sorry about all of this," he continued. "I only intended to help when I heard about your accident. Not scare ya. But don't ya worry. That spell will wear off within hours."

Chapter Six

Elodie peeked around the edge of a bookshelf. The dark wood was anchored to the wall of an ornate library—almost too ornate. Something happened when wealthy people were left alone with all their money. Everything became more prominent and more glamorous to the point of painfully gaudy. It was like the time her mother decided to decorate the foyer with Greek statues under giant metal coconut tree sculptures. Cost a fortune and looked like a meth addict had gotten ahold of her credit card.

Elodie wasn't sure why her mother was in her head. Maybe she needed to cling to something normal. Perhaps it was more to do with the hurt she felt when the woman couldn't even bother to talk to her on the phone. Home and family were supposed to be safe places. Elodie really needed a safe place.

The tweed-clad spokesman from the bedroom's back was to her. He moved like he was in conversation with a ghost, but the sound of his voice had suddenly stopped, taking ambient noises with it. She rubbed her fingers by her ear, unable to hear a soft noise. She thought about trying something louder but didn't want the host to find her. Who knew how he would react? The zombie farmers hadn't been welcoming. Her sore face could attest to that.

Seeing a door, she tried crawling toward it. Her hand reached out, hoping it would slowly push open so she could sneak through unnoticed. There had to be a way out of this hell.

Before she could make contact, the wooden door swung forward. She darted out of the way as bare legs passed by. When the door shut in front of her, it had transformed into thin, dented metal.

"You can't be back here, sugar. Mack don't like it none," a thick Southern accent scolded.

Elodie glanced up to find a bouffant-coifed waitress sloppily chewing gum as she stared down at her. She held her pencil like a weapon, at the ready to take an order.

"Uh, sorry," Elodie muttered, forcing herself to stand up from behind a counter.

The library was gone, and she stood in a busy 1950s-style diner. Classic cars drove slowly past the window, and a woman in a button-down shirt dress strode with two young children in tow.

Inside the diner, booths filled with a combination of loud teenagers and their more subdued opposites. Crooners emanated ballads from the jukebox. When Elodie looked back at the waitress, the woman was eyeing her attire in a combination of confusion and disgust. By the crowd, plaid pajama pants and t-shirts were not yet popular.

Snakes. Sand. Paralyzed. Zombies. Hockey. Time travel?

Elodie leaned closer to the waitress and asked, "Do you know what's— "

All sound suddenly stopped. She gasped, leaning back. It wasn't just the sound. It was movement. The waitress stood frozen before her.

Elodie looked around in panic. A grizzled man's face stared through a passthrough from the kitchen. He, too, had stopped moving, as had the diners and the vehicles outside.

She heard her feet on the laminate tiles, so at least there was sound this time, even if she was the only person making it.

She looked at the waitress's nametag. "Bobbi Sue?"

The waitress didn't answer. She was like looking at a wax figurine.

Elodie moved around the counter toward the booths. The teens were frozen in laughter as a boy tried to shove an entire hamburger into his mouth. The older couple behind them looked amused by the antics.

"Hello?" she called, waving her hand in front of a girl's face. "Is anyone here?"

Nothing.

Elodie tried to leave. Bells jingled as she shook the door, but it refused to let her out. She rushed to push the metal kitchen door. It swung open easily. She hurried past the cook, watching to see if he'd turn to yell at her. He didn't.

Hamburgers waited on the grill mid-sizzle. The drip from a spill held suspended as it reached for the floor. It was then she realized smells had been suspended too. The typical diner aroma of hot grease no longer filled the air.

Seeing a back door, she ran for it. The knob turned, but it wouldn't open. She jammed her shoulder against it.

"I don't understand this game," she yelled. Was this a game? Video game? One of those escape rooms? Did she have to search for clues to get out? "I didn't sign up for this. Please, I want to leave."

Again nothing.

"Ok. Ok. Think, Elodie." She looked around for clues. She'd always been good at coming up with scenarios and solving mysteries before the end of the show. "Diner. People go to diners for food. Maybe this is saying it's my chance to eat something?"

The rationalization wasn't comforting. If she was supposed to dine, then that indicated she was in for the long haul. Her stomach churned in protest at the idea of putting anything in her mouth.

"I don't understand," she whispered. "I don't know what I'm supposed to do. I don't know why I'm here."

She began searching the kitchen, pulling open drawers and refrigerators. Panic mounted. How could it not?

Elodie neared Chef Grizzled and lightly patted his pockets while staring at his immobile expression. Aside from a pack of cigarettes, they were empty.

She pushed through the metal door, walking along the booths as she stared into the motionless faces. She checked inside jacket pockets and a woman's purse. She frantically searched behind the counter and tried to open the register. She angled her head to see everything outside the windows. She read the shorthand on the waitress's notepad, but it was only a food order.

"What do you want with me?" She screamed into Bobbi Sue's face. She hit the woman on the arm, but it was like slapping a steel plate.

Elodie grabbed a plate off the counter and launched it at the wall. It made a satisfying crash, so she hurled a second one after it.

"Someone answer me!" She screamed louder, moving from stiff face to stiff face, trying to make the customers notice her. She poked the older man's hand with a fork. She dumped the woman's purse on the table to provoke a reaction. She dumped a milkshake on a teenager's head. "What do you want with me?"

Nothing happened. The statues didn't care.

Elodie sat on a barstool and lowered her head to the counter. Tears filled her eyes, and she tried to keep them from dripping onto her arm. She was afraid to look up in case the world changed again but also frightened that it would stay the same.

"Please," she whispered, begging an unseen force. "I don't understand."

A light scratching sound caught her attention in the silence. She lifted off the stool to see what made the noise. The sound came from overhead, and she looked at an erased chalkboard that had listed lunch specials moments before.

Words formed as an invisible hand wrote in chalk, "*Who are you?*"

"I'm..." She glanced around. Nothing else had changed. "My name is Elodie. Elodie Fairweather. One second..."

She searched behind the counter for chalk, wondering if she had to write her answer.

The scratches sounded again. She looked up. The first question had been erased, and the chalk writing spelled out, "*How did you get in there?*"

"I don't know. It's like I'm on a television set, and someone is flipping channels. One second, I was in my motel room. Then things got hazy and weird, and I felt like I was wrapped in a tight blanket while people tried to talk to me. The next I was traveling through..." She looked at the frozen patrons wondering to whom she was speaking. "Who are you? Where are you? Can you see me?"

The chalk wrote, "*Bruce MacGregor. Hotel Motel. On TV.*"

"How are you communicating like this, Bruce?" Elodie again looked around. Was this some trick?

The word erased itself, and a single dot

appeared as if he hesitated to write. Finally, he answered, "*Magick.*"

"Magick," she repeated, wanting to be skeptical but unable to muster the disbelief such a statement would usually cause. Was any other explanation more reasonable? Well, besides the idea that she was in a locked ward under a doctor's supervision. "How is this possible?"

He answered, "*Spell side effect?*"

"Question mark. So you're not sure," she reasoned. "Did you pause it?"

"*Aye. I won't change the channel.*"

She looked at the frozen people. "Thank you. This is better than lions and zombies."

"*Are you magick?*"

Elodie couldn't help a small laugh. She shook her head. "No. I'm a spoiled heiress rebelling against her parents' insipid lifestyle. How do I get out of here?"

Again there was a pause before the chalked answer appeared. "*Time.*"

"How much time?"

"*Unsure.*"

Elodie sat on a different stool and lifted a lid to a pie cover. Leaning over to sniff it, she frowned at the lack of scent. "Think I can eat in here?"

He underlined the word *Unsure*.

"Am I crazy? This feels like a hallucination. It

must be." She stared at the chalkboard. Nothing changed. "Are you still there? Bruce?"

Elodie didn't want him to leave her. He was the first ray of hope she'd found since the craziness started.

"*Yes.*"

A wave of dizziness came over her like blasts of cold and heat warring over her skin, and she held her forehead. Her nerves tingled as if zapped with electricity before starting to subside. "I think I'm going to be sick."

The wave hit her again, harder, and she trembled.

"This isn't right."

She glanced up for his answer. There was none.

"Bruce? Please, don't leave."

"*Trying to get you out.*"

The rush of nausea hit her again, sending an ache through her bones. Tears came to her eyes, and she closed them tight as she hugged her arms around her stomach. "Ah. Stop!"

The pain stopped.

Elodie gasped for breath. "Whatever you're doing, it's not working."

When she opened her eyes, Bobbi Sue stood in front of her. The waitress's face was frozen mid-angry word.

"They moved," Elodie said, searching the other patrons to find their creepy statues peering in her direction. Their silent stares caused her to change to a different seat, so they weren't looking at her.

"*You're safe.*"

She wanted to believe him, but he was only magickal words written on a specials board in a 1950s diner. "Why is this happening to me? Did I do something wrong?"

He circled the word *safe*.

She wanted to believe him. She also wanted to keep him talking.

"So, are you, um, magickal?" She gave a derisive laugh and waved her hand. "Never mind. Of course, you are. You're…" She motioned at the chalkboard.

"*Warlock.*"

"Warlock? Like a male witch?"

The words "*No a*" appeared before *Warlock*.

"No, you're a warlock, not a witch. Like…?" Elodie vaguely recalled a movie where warlocks were evil, but a 1980s horror movie felt like a poor point for factual reference. The last thing she wanted was to insult the one person who seemed to know what was happening. "So this spell? Is that like a curse? Is that why all these bad things are happening? Someone is trying to kill me?"

"*Believe unintentional.*"

The words were erased quickly.

"*What bad things?*"

Elodie stared at the board, trying to imagine the face and voice of the man she talked to. The image of the man talking on the phone outside her room, with his Scottish accent, came to mind. As did the blurry face that had hovered over her while she lay trapped on the bed. She found herself answering, telling him in detail about the snake and the sand, and then finding herself at the motel when she'd been at a rest stop. When she finished, she said, "I heard someone outside. I went to look, and then I felt like I was drugged while people talked over me. I tried so hard to move, and when I finally did, I was…"

Elodie gestured to encompass the television prison.

A bell jingled, and she caught movement from the corner of her eye. She spun toward it. A paused man stood holding his hat in one hand and the door open with the other. The diner figures had moved into new positions. The teenager stood with the milkshake dripping off him. The older woman stared at her purse contents in dismay. The waitress glared and clenched a fist. The menacing cook was halfway out of the kitchen, holding a knife.

"Bruce?"

The sound of chalk drew her attention upward. "*Run.*"

"I…" Elodie glanced at the cook before hurrying toward the now-opened door.

She pushed her hand through the barrier, ensuring it wasn't magickally blocked. Ducking beneath his arm, she made her way outside. Though bright, she couldn't feel the heat of sunlight on her skin. Tree leaves held to the side, but she couldn't hear the breeze crashing through the unmoving leaves.

"It's like a dead world," she whispered, making her way down the sidewalk and across a street toward the town square. A classic Merc sat in the way, mid-drive. When she looked inside, the man's face was blurred.

Her legs felt heavy as she neared the curb, and she instinctively knew whatever magick held her in this place did not want her exploring outside of the current television screen.

"Bruce?" She searched for a sign from him. The distant street blurred into streaks of color. Seeing a tree next to a courthouse, she sat beside it, hoping to blend in so the angry diners didn't come for her. "Can you hear me? I can't run. This place won't let me."

As if to answer her, a blast of sound punctuated the air. She peeked to see the cook on the sidewalk, holding his knife.

"Don't un-pause it," she begged, hoping Bruce could hear her.

What if he'd been toying with her?

What if he was the cause of this?

Did she have a choice but to trust him?

Sound blasted again, brief and loud, and it caused her to jolt in fright. She glanced again. The cook stood near the Merc, his legs indicating he was coming for her, as the driver pointed in her direction.

Elodie pushed up from the ground and ran toward the blurry distance. The closer she got, the harder it became to move. She turned course, hurrying toward the side of the diner to press tight against the wall. The sound blasted again, and she saw the cook had made it across the street, near where she had been. Seconds later, a short shout sounded, and he was coming back toward her mid-run.

"Bruce?" she whispered, leaning to glance inside the diner window.

Her eyes went up to the chalkboard. "*Change channel?*"

Sound started, but this time it didn't stop. The figures moved. Chaos sounded inside the diner as patrons rushed the window. The cook ran toward

Elodie. Back inside, she found Bobbi Sue blocking her way when she tried to go to the only place she could.

"Yes!" Elodie screamed as she stumbled away from the door to run from the cook. "Change it. Change it!"

Her legs became heavy before someone shoved her hard in the back. Suddenly the ground was no longer under her feet as she fell out of an airplane into the open sky. Others dropped around her, but they all had parachutes and protective gear. Elodie screamed, frantically searching her clothes as the freezing air hit her bare skin. She watched the ground come closer and could do nothing about it. She closed her eyes and gritted her teeth, bracing for impact and knowing she wouldn't survive it.

Instead of the hard earth, her body became encased in cold water. Salt stung her eyes and flooded her mouth as a shadowy figure swam past. Seconds later, she was dripping wet on dry land, being pelted by desert sand as the wind swept a barren landscape. The intense heat dried her clothes. Before she could catch her breath, two street racers swept along either side of her in a cityscape. She screamed and blocked her face.

"Shush!"

Elodie lowered her shaking arms and found herself standing in a library.

"Quiet," a librarian warned in a harsh whisper and even harsher finger point. Several people looked up from their laptops and books in irritation.

"Sorry," she mouthed, backing away from them to hide behind a bookshelf. "Bruce, if you can hear me, stop. Here is good."

She swiped at the sand adhering to her skin, brushing it off onto the floor. The dirt stung her eyes, but there was little she could do about that. She would have felt bad about the mess, but this was a fake world inside a magickal television.

Elodie grabbed a book from the shelf and went to an empty, cushioned chair along a back wall. Sinking down, she pulled the book open and held it in front of her like a shield as she surveyed her surroundings. A cold chill flowed over her, but she ignored it.

"Don't change the channel," she whispered, pulling her legs up onto the seat to hunch over as small as she could make herself. "This place seems safe enough for now."

She glanced around for a sign that Bruce had heard her. She stared at the book in her hands, seeing the words but not really reading them as she watched for changes to the walls of text.

Time. He had said that an unsure amount of time was how she got out of there. So all she had to do was wait.

But for how long? An hour was much different than years. It already felt like she'd been inside this not-so-funhouse of magick for at least a day, maybe longer. How did one mark time inside a television program?

What if she got hungry? Or tired? Or needed to use a restroom?

Would any of that be safe? Pausing had only worked for so long at the diner before the cook decided to chase after her with a knife. It might have had something to do with her dumping milk-shakes on his customers and rifling purses, but still, it had been an overreaction.

What if Bruce couldn't continue to communicate with her?

What if the scene on this show changed out of the library like it had during the museum tour?

"I hate this," she whispered, unable to help feeling sorry for herself.

What had she done to deserve this? Sure, she wasn't a perfect human, but she wasn't bad, let alone evil. She didn't steal or kill things. She didn't hate strangers for no reason. She supported animal shelters and other charities. She was trying to write a book that kept changing from fiction to a road memoir, à la Steinbeck's *Travels with Charley*. Seeing how this trip was going, no one would believe any of her misadventures to be true. And being trapped inside a television sounded like lousy fiction. Who would ever believe this?

Elodie glanced up from her book and looked pointedly around the room. The patrons turned pages with consistent regularity as if their job title was something like Library Student Number Two.

In the relative safety of the library chair, her mind began to run wild. Another chill worked over her, and she burrowed deeper into the cushions.

Her parents were wealthy. Could this be a kidnapping? Would Janelle even answer the phone if the kidnappers called? Elodie knew her father wouldn't. The man tended to forget he had a family until a photo op was needed for some magazine spread touting his awesomeness or a Who's Who Christmas party charade.

Serial killer? Nah, this felt a little too hands-off for them.

Roofie? No, she'd be unconscious, right?

Military experiment? Like the MKUltra thing where they drugged unsuspecting citizens.

Mental ward? Ok, yeah, sure, at this point in the story, that fit.

Magickal warlock holding her prisoner with a

spell—*accidental or not remained to be seen*? Strangely, that was the closest answer she had to the truth, and it was the most insane option. To accept that meant several things. Warlocks were real. Magick was real. Spells existed and could be cast. Zombies could be summoned, so surely that meant other things could be manifested.

Another chill came over her. This time it lingered.

Elodie felt a strange prickling against her arm and slowly turned her head toward the aisle between the back wall and endcaps of bookshelves. A transparent figure hovered a few feet away. The end of her long twentieth-century dress and feet were missing, but she moved as if she walked.

Elodie turned her face toward the book and pretended to read as the ghost neared. The temperature dropped. Her hands shook, and it was all she could do to hold onto the book.

Around the edges of the hardback, she saw the faded end of the dress pause in front of the chair. A hand came forward to hover over the page. Elodie remained frozen in place, holding her breath. The fingers flexed and curled as if searching for a reaction.

Suddenly a scream came from where the

others quietly read. The ghost snatched her hand away and whisked toward the noise.

Elodie let go of her breath. The book dropped, and she panted in fear as the screams became punctuated by the sounds of crashing bookshelves and strange thuds. A man flew past her line of vision and knocked into the wall. He fell unconscious to the ground.

Elodie stood and tried to tiptoe down the aisle, away from the angry spirit. Suddenly, the ghost was there, staring at her, shoulders hunched and face contorted with rage.

"Ah, come on," Elodie muttered. The woman was spending the afterlife in a library. How angry could she actually be?

The ghost surged forward, preceded by a blast of cold air. Her high-pitched screech was enough to make her ears bleed.

"Bruce, channel!" Elodie yelled, trying to run.

Her feet tripped as icy fingers grabbed her arms and lifted her into the air. For a transparent body, the ghost had a decidedly firm grip. Elodie was released and launched upward.

She braced for impact. Instead of hitting a wall, she fell to a marble floor, "Umph," and slid a few feet.

Chapter Seven

Elodie looked up at the ceiling from the ground. The library ceiling was gone, and a gaudy chandelier replaced the fluorescent lights. She suppressed a cough as she tried to regain her breath. The height of the ceiling combined with the elaborate open staircase with polished wood railing reminded her of foyers in wealthy old homes she'd visited with her parents.

"What the fuck now?" she managed, half groaning, half grumbling. "Dr. Frankenstein's mansion? Supervillain's lair? Private spa with my mother?"

All sounded like versions of hell.

Elodie couldn't get the willpower to move, so she stayed on the unforgivingly hard floor, exhausted.

"There she is," a thick Scottish accent declared. "Our noisy mystery guest. What can I do for ya, lassie?"

A man's grinning face appeared over where she lay. Survival instinct kicked in. She rolled away from him while scrambling to her hands and knees.

The man wore a worn kilt and a t-shirt that offered free mustache rides. His hair was wet, and he smelled of sandalwood. He didn't appear to be the same man she'd seen hovering over her in the motel room, but he seemed to be expecting her.

"Bruce?" Elodie asked.

"Och, no, lassie!" The man grimaced as if she'd flung a dead fish at him. "I'm much better looking than Bruce. My poor nephew is better compared to Frankenstein's monster and not my fine specimen of masculinity, don't ya think?"

"I don't…" Elodie shook her head in confusion.

"Ya can call me Raibeart," the man said. He stood barefoot on the marble. The house said he was rich. The naked feet and t-shirt choice said he was playfully eccentric.

She looked down, seeing she was in no position to judge his attire. She was still barefoot and in dirty, damp pajama pants.

"Or Dr. Frankenstein, if ya prefer," he added when she didn't readily speak.

"Is this place…"

"For sale?" Raibeart guessed when she didn't finish. "Hard to clean? Full of Gremians? Not anymore."

"Uh, monster, Frankenstein…"

"Ya said Frankenstein mansion first," Raibeart noted. "Not the funniest of jokes, but ya look like ya had a rough time of it, so I let the lack of humor slide. Though, I wouldn't say that joke to Cait. She's proud of her decorating. I personally voted that we add more color. White is so sterile."

"Cait?" Elodie hazily recalled a woman introducing herself as Cait when she'd been paralyzed in the hotel room.

"Bruce's ma," Raibeart supplied. He eyed her crouched on the ground. "Come up off the floor. This isn't the audition for Cats, though ya do look a bit feral."

"So, I'm out of the television?" She took a deep breath as she pushed to her feet. "This is real again?"

"Yeah, been there." Raibeart laughed. "Tricky gadgets, aren't they? Wait, no, I'm thinking of a cursed escalator. The thing had me trapped for three hours."

"How many times do I have to tell ya, Uncle

Raibeart, it wasn't cursed?" Another kilted man came from an adjoining room. Behind him, a formal dining table and chairs were neatly set. He held a muffin in one hand and bit into the top. With a mouth full, he added, "Ya were drunk and standing on a concrete stairwell."

"Didn't we marry ya off, Euann? Aren't ya supposed to move out of the house at some point like a big boy?" Raibeart asked.

"You're one to talk," Euann grumbled.

Raibeart wiggled his fingers as Euann tried to take another bite. Euann's hand twitched, and he shoved the muffin against his own nose.

Raibeart laughed and motioned for Elodie to walk with him toward where Euann had appeared with the food. "Come get a bite, love."

Elodie didn't move.

"Hey, are ya Melody, by chance?" Euann asked, dropping muffin crumbs as he swiped at his nose.

"Elodie," she answered.

"Right. That's it. Elodie. Bruce called looking for ya. He sounded frantic going on about some girl getting sucked into a television and then disappearing." Euann grinned. "Playing games with him, aye?"

"I don't…" She shook her head.

"So, who put ya up to it?" Euann asked. "Maura? Rory? Erik?"

"I...?" She again shook her head in confusion.

"Neat trick." Euann's expression turned thoughtful. "I'm going to have to rethink my strategy."

"Strategy?" Elodie found herself asking.

Euann grinned. "Aye. For setting up my cousin. He's the last bachelor standing—well, wait, that's not technically right, being as Raibeart had kids popping out of the netherworld."

A setup?

Elodie did not return his smile. She felt anger flooding her body as every muscle started to clench. "Trapping me inside bad television programming is a joke to you?"

Euann instantly frowned. "Wait, no, I didn't—"

She touched her sore cheek where she'd been punched, right beneath her desert-irritated eye, and winced.

"That bruise is real?" Euann tried to ask.

The rage exploded as she talked over him. "You're lucky I am not magickal, or else I'd see how you like being punched in the face by zombie bait, and drowned in sand, and thrown around by ghosts, and tossed out of airplanes without a chute, and snakes, and dirty cooks, and pizza commercials, and gorillas, and—"

"Easy—" Euann held up his hand and tried to soothe her.

"Easy? You think that was easy?" Elodie yelled.

"I meant take it easy. Calm down. It will be all right. No one wants ya—"

"I got to get out of here." Elodie searched around frantically until her brain was able to process the front door. She hurried toward it, praying it would open and let her out.

"Hey, wait, don't go Elodie. I had no idea this was real for ya. I thought—"

The door opened, and she ran outside.

"Ah, look what ya did," Raibeart scolded Euann, his voice following her.

"Me? I…" Euann started to protest.

Elodie moved faster. The cobblestone drive against her bare feet made walking uncomfortable, but she didn't care. She needed to escape. A town came into view at the bottom of a hill. She passed sports cars parked in the driveway as she followed the route down.

When she glanced back to see if she was followed, she found instead a giant Georgian-style mansion towering over the lawn, surrounded by a forest that ran down the sides of the hill. It was then she realized it was daytime. She must have been trapped in the television world for hours. The front door remained open, but she didn't see anyone watching her.

Elodie kept moving, intent on running, as she turned back toward the path. Her toes jammed into something hard, and she yelped as she fell forward onto the steps. She grabbed her foot as she moaned in pain. The mansion's stairs had reappeared, and she found herself at the opened door.

"Muffin?" Raibeart offered her the baked good on top of a napkin.

Elodie kept hold of her foot. "Please, let me go."

"Where would ya like to go?" he asked as if this were the most normal of situations. He tossed the muffin over his shoulder into the foyer. "We'll steal any car ya want. Oh, might I suggest the Leprechaun naked run in Oklahoma? Tuscan cliff diving? Perhaps a pizza downtown? You'll have to go in to order. I've been banned. Again."

Her foot throbbed, and the last thing she wanted was an adventure.

The sound of car tires throwing gravel as an engine burred angrily up the driveway kept her from answering. She turned on the steps, still holding her foot as she watched the dust flying over the landscape. An old blue Corvette burst onto the cobblestone in a billowing dust cloud.

She felt the panic inside of her calming.

"Does this mean no pizza?" Raibeart sounded disappointed.

The car skidded to a stop. Elodie dropped her foot and stood, no longer feeling the pain.

She knew him the moment he stepped out of the car. "Bruce."

He rushed around the car to get to her, leaving the driver's door open. She recognized his paint-splattered jeans and old t-shirt from outside the hotel.

"Elodie." His hands lifted as if he would touch her face, but he stopped himself. Concerned green eyes stared into hers. Overgrown strands of hair framed his face. If the dark circles under his eyes were any indication, it looked as if he hadn't slept. "Ya made it out."

"Thank you for changing the channel."

"I tried to use magick to get ya out faster, to send ya to safety. I was worried I'd failed when ya disappeared from the motel." Bruce's hand lifted, this time as if to touch hers. He again stopped himself.

"I don't know how I got here. I don't know where here is." She felt they were being watched, and she glanced at Raibeart. The man didn't even try to hide his interest in what they were doing.

"This is my family's home," Bruce explained. "You're safe here."

"So your magick worked? It's over?" A strand of hair tickled her cheek, and she moved to brush it aside. Her fingers found a patch of dirt adhered to her temple. She frowned as she realized how bad she probably looked.

"We were discussing running naked with Leprechauns if ya care to join us," Raibeart said.

"We're not doing that," Bruce dismissed.

"Ya can paint yourself green again," Raibeart enticed.

"Uncle Raibeart, can ya give us a moment?" Bruce moved as if to block Raibeart from her view.

"Oh, aye, don't want your Uncle Raibeart stealing all the attention. I get it, laddie," Raibeart answered.

Elodie leaned to watch him go inside. Raibeart left the door open. Seeing the foyer, she said, "You live here?"

"No. Never. Some of my extended family members do—aunts, uncles, cousins, my brother, their spouses—at some point or another, the extended family moves in and out. I prefer to stay away from the crazy in the motel."

Considering what just happened in the motel, Elodie found that statement to be not strictly rational.

"I used my magick to send ya someplace safe. I thought it would be the motel, but this is where ya appeared," he said. "Ya have to be exhausted. There are plenty of guest rooms inside. Why don't we find ya one?"

"I'm not sure…" She didn't know what to do. With all the strangeness happening, events she couldn't explain, she knew she had no choice but to trust him. Bruce made her feel safe, safer than she had in a long time. "All right. Yes. Thank you."

Bruce gestured toward his car. The driver-side door slammed shut without anyone touching it. She stiffened and stared at it for a moment. The logical part of her brain told her none of this could be real.

"The house is protected by magick. My cousin has barrier spells on the property and around the house. The one good thing about an extended family home is there are always warlocks around ready to protect ya." Bruce gave a small laugh. "The bad thing about an extended family home is there are always warlocks around."

"Do you know what spell caused my uh," she

hesitated as he walked with her up the front steps, "television appearance?"

Bruce didn't touch her though his hand hovered in her direction like he wanted to. "I can't be sure, but I think it might be our fault. My family has been setting me up on blind dates. I didn't ask them to, but they're meddlesome. I think maybe one of their pranks went awry, and ya were caught in the mischief."

He let her step through the door first. A trail of crumbs led to Raibeart's discarded muffin. Euann's squished muffin remained where he had dropped it.

"Ugh, sorry about the mess," Bruce grumbled when he saw her staring at it. He waved his hand, and the muffins swept themselves into a pile before lifting and floating out of the room.

"How are you doing that?" Elodie took a deep breath.

"Magick," he answered.

"But what is *that*? How? Can anyone learn?" She lifted her hand and mimicked his gestures. Nothing happened. "Is it like some kind of Las Vegas show trade secret thing?"

"Magic-no-k is what ya think of when ya think of sawing someone in half or making them disappear. Magick-with-a-ck is founded on something ancient, something real. Families like mine evolved in a way that allows us to harness it." Bruce held out his hand, and blue flames appeared as a sphere on this palm. "Think of it as a trade, a transfer of energy. I borrow a little bit of energy from somewhere else in order to produce the energy needed to make something happen."

"Somewhere else?"

"Life force. Energy. Plant life, people, other activities," he said. "Usually, we just take a little, not enough for the plants to notice. At worst, if we went unchecked, we could kill an entire forest."

She gestured her hand again, seeing if she could create flames.

"Here." He rolled the magick ball into her hand. It tingled against her palm, sending intense sensations up the nerves of her arm before dissipating.

"I promise to answer all the questions I can, but I think ya should rest. You'll be safe here." He motioned toward the long staircase. "Guest suites are up there."

Elodie considered her options. Part of her wanted to go back to the motel, but nowhere felt safe. Finally, following his suggestion, she decided to stay.

She watched her feet on the wide tread marble steps and held onto the rail. Tired muscles caused her to walk slowly. "How long has your family lived here? Did your ancestors come over from Scotland and build it?"

"No. We've been in Wisconsin for only a handful of years. There used to be a lot more of us living in the same area. We move around quite a bit, and over the decades, members of the MacGregor clan have remained in other states. I have extended-extended family all over the world. My ma could tell ya more. She knows everyone, all the twelfth cousins thrice removed." He gave a small laugh. "Honestly, at this point, I just consider it best not to date another warlock. Ya never know if they're some distant branch of the family line."

"So this place is not like a *family home*-family home," she said, reaching the top landing. She paused to look down on the foyer. She saw movement in the doorway Euann had appeared from earlier with his muffin. The edge of the dining room table was empty, though. Whoever it was, they were hiding and eavesdropping. "It's a new family home."

"I suppose."

"How big is it?" She watched the dining room.

Bruce followed her gaze. "Uh, I think they said eighty-some acres forest, five or six acres of gardens, twenty thousand square foot house, sixty or seventy rooms, roughly. My cousin Erik could probably tell ya more accurate information."

"Servants on staff?" She saw the edge of an arm appear.

"None."

"Really?" She glanced back to look at him. She'd never known a home this large to be without staff—cooks, maids, gardeners, nannies, pool boys, personal assistants, security... Janelle Fairweather would have been lost without a team to help her run her homes.

He gave a small cleaning gesture of his hand. "Don't need them."

Another peek of the eavesdropper's arm showed.

Bruce sighed and pointed toward the dining room. A stream of yellow shot out of his finger.

"*Hey*—" Euann's voice was cut off as his arm swung forward and stopped moving. He held very still, like a statue.

"If anyone asks, ya didn't see me do that," Bruce said.

"Is he...?" Elodie started moving back downstairs to get a better look.

"Petrifying spell. He'll thaw out in a few hours," Bruce answered. "He should learn to mind his own business. Now, I'm sorry, ya were saying?"

Elodie stared for a moment longer before returning to the landing. Somehow seeing Bruce's powers didn't frighten her as they would have a few days ago. After traveling through TV world, she found comfort in the idea that someone could harness and control the magick. "You live and work at the motel?"

"It's all part of the local MacGregor Empire."

"Empire. That sounds intimidating. What kind of empire? Are you motel moguls?" Elodie knew it was sometimes considered gauche to ask how wealthy people made their money. She also knew that many people with money secretly loved to talk about it. Bruce didn't appear to be one of the bragging types, but she was still getting to know him.

"Not just motels. I run the motel with my sister, Maura. I have a twin brother, Rory, who is in Europe doing who-knows-what. He was supposed to help us. My cousin Iain and his wife have the plant nursery. Euann and his wife just opened the new library. Raibeart's pet project is literally pets. He's taken over the animal shelter. His wife helps out there. She's had a rough time of it and is still adjusting to, uh, modern life. Maura's husband, Jefferson, owns a pub restaurant. I highly recommend it. Niall has an apartment building downtown, but he's never here.

Erik and his wife have a girly-lotion-candle business called Love Potions. The family elders run
corporations all over the world. Basically, if there
is a business to buy, we buy it." He took a couple
of steps down a hallway and paused for her to
join him.

Elodie fell into step next to him. The landing
split off into two directions. Each hallway hosted
rows of closed doors. "That's a lot of businesses.
And everyone in town? They know what—I mean
who—you are? They must, right?"

"No. It's kind of one of the supernatural rules.
We don't advertise that we exist. It's the one thing
we all seem to agree on. Humans haven't always
handled the news well." Bruce stopped at the door
at the end and knocked. They waited, but no one
inside answered. He opened it and led the way
inside.

"And when you say *the supernatural,* you
mean…?"

He gave a small laugh. "When I promised to
answer all your questions, I meant after ya rest. I
feel like we're getting into some big topics."

The room carried the old-world wood theme
that decorated the rest of the house. Half panels
lined the walls and gave focus to a large fireplace.
Candelabras were spaced along the mantle. Over

the fireplace was a painting of a castle along a cliff.

"Bathroom is there. I'll leave ya to it and be back with food and a change of clothes." Bruce reached for the door and started to pull it closed, only to stop. "You're safe here. I promise no one in this house will want to do ya harm. I won't be gone long."

"Thank you." Elodie turned toward the bathroom as she listened to the door close. She took a deep breath and let it out slowly. This was not how she pictured this trip going. She'd run away from mansions and people with money and never expected to find herself back surrounded by that lavish lifestyle.

The bed looked inviting, but it would be rude to fall into it in her disheveled state. Crossing to the bathroom, she found towels and a plush robe next to a jet-lined tub. A shelf filled with toiletries had anticipated every possible need. She saw that the labels on most of the bottles read, "*Love Potions.*"

Everything was rich and lavish and perfect. It was everything she had tried to get away from.

"Be grateful for what you have. Many people have nothing," Elodie whispered as she started the bath, wishing she was back in the roadside motel.

Chapter Eight

Bruce sat guard over Elodie as she slept. The food tray he'd brought was on the mantle next to the candelabras. She'd been asleep when he returned, her body splayed out on the top of the comforter as she wore a robe. He hoped she enjoyed the luxury. To him, this was just a place like any other place. He'd been in rooms like this off and on his whole life. He preferred the motel. People acted differently to him when he lived in a motel than when he lived in a mansion.

Sitting in a chair, he studied her beautiful face. It had taken everything in him not to touch her. His nerves screamed that they knew her, yet they had never met before now.

Bruce lifted his hand and summoned the flames. The fireplace lit. It wasn't cold, but he wanted to see the orange reflecting off her features. With another gesture, he materialized his sketchpad and charcoal. He drew the outline of her form, the soft sweep of her cheek leading to the fluffy bumps of the robe. His eyes stared at her as his hand moved. He wanted to get everything exact so he could recall this moment centuries from now.

Her lips were parted with breath, and he knew he could never capture the soft rise and fall of her back. No artist could do her justice. No drawing could relay how he felt watching her at this moment. At best, he could hope for a pretty picture.

Bruce stopped drawing, leaving it unfinished. He dropped the pad and charcoal on the floor by his feet.

Magick lazily danced along his fingertips, slithering like a snake between the digits before winding up his arm and over his shoulder. He tried to untangle his emotions. He felt attraction. He wanted to touch her soft skin, but at the same time, he didn't want to disturb the view.

There were very few events in life where he wanted to live in a moment forever. This was one of them. He could be happy here, in his chair, watching Elodie sleep, hypnotized by her breathing.

"Where did ya come from, lassie?" he whispered, not wanting an answer.

It occurred to him that he might be under a spell, some prank cast by a family member to make him want to date. He found he didn't care. It was better than the footage he saw of his cousin, Erik, under the influence of a love potion prank. That had been horrifically painful to watch. Erik had been dancing and singing on his now-wife's front lawn like a wood sprite after it found a barrel of ale. Bruce would do anything for his cousin...except listen to him give a concert.

The magickal snake wound around his neck before slithering off his arm. He let it drop off his fingers onto the sketchpad.

Elodie gave a small moan. The robe over her leg shifted and moved, but her leg stayed still.

Bruce frowned, instantly standing to get a better look at what was happening. The material moved like a snake traveled beneath it. The robe inched up her calf to reveal healing puncture wounds. He glanced at the floor. His magickal snake was slithering over her portrait, mimicking the movement beneath the robe.

Bruce instantly smothered the magick, and the movement beneath the robe stopped. He watched closely for several minutes.

He materialized another snake and dropped it

on her portrait. Instantly, the robe began to move again, and he smothered the second one.

Bruce carefully picked up the sketchpad. The blurry streaks of two scorched snakes joined the image of Elodie in the drawing. This was a strange development.

He gently shut the book and placed it on the mantle where it would be safe. When he moved to take his seat, it was to find Elodie awake and looking at him. She sat up on the bed and held her robe closed.

"How are ya feeling?" he asked, keeping his voice soft as he was loath to break the quiet spell of emotion she had cast over him.

"Strange dreams," she answered. "Almost nightmares, actually."

"I'm sorry to hear that," he said.

Elodie pulled up her robe and looked at the puncture wounds on her leg. She suppressed a yawn. "This is where the snake I was telling you about bit me. I was dreaming that it was back and crawling over me."

Bruce gave a guilty glance at the sketchpad and saw the food tray.

"I brought ya something to eat." He grabbed the tray and set it next to her on the bed. It was an assortment of muffins, a sandwich, and a bag of chips. "I was trying to hurry. If ya want something else, name it. I'll get it for ya."

"Mm." She opened the chips and took the top slice of bread off the sandwich. "This is perfect."

Bruce watched her pile a layer of chips into the sandwich before replacing the top slice. She smashed it down and then lifted it and took a bite.

"Interesting," he said.

"Gourmet." Elodie winked and took another bite. "So good."

Bruce laughed and sat on the edge of the bed. He reached over to grab the bag of chips and helped himself. He liked that she seemed easy to please and wasn't demanding.

She tore off a corner and handed it to him. "Try it."

He laughed as he took it from her. Their fingers brushed. They'd come close when he handed her the ball of magick, but this was the first time they touched. He felt the shock of it more powerful than all the magick he could summons.

Her smile dropped a little as she stared at him. Their fingers lingered, the tickling caress hanging between them before she slowly pulled away first.

Bruce popped the sandwich piece into his mouth and made a show of crunching it. He laughed and nodded. "You're right. Potato chip sandwiches are good."

"It drives my parents crazy to watch me eat. My mom is all health shakes and fad diets. My dad preaches health while sneaking cigarettes, bourbon, and steaks with his friends." Elodie reached into the bag to take more chips and shoved them inside her meal. "You know what else is good? Fast food French fries on hamburgers."

"I'm seeing a theme with ya." He enjoyed watching her.

Elodie pulled at her robe, closing the neck higher. "French fries dipped in chocolate milkshakes."

She gave a light shrug and continued eating as if perfectly content in the moment.

Bruce again looked at the pad. He didn't want to spoil her mood, but he also wanted to be honest. "I may have a clue as to what's causing your bad luck."

She stopped midbite and lowered the sand-wich to the tray. "Oh?"

Bruce went to retrieve the pad. "When I was watching ya sleep, I discovered something."

"Oh?" This time the word sounded more worried.

He sat back down and opened the sketchpad. "I think the spell has something to do with my drawings. And not just the drawing, maybe paintings, and just all of it."

Elodie stared at him, clearly not understanding. She self-consciously wiped at crumbs alongside her mouth even though he didn't see any.

"You mentioned you were bit by a snake. I had been painting one of the motel room walls with a portrait of Echidna."

"En-what?"

"Echidna," he repeated.

"Aren't those like hedgehogs? I don't understand. A hedgehog cursed me?" Her brow furrowed.

"Not that kind of Echidna. She's a half-snake, half-woman who favors living in cave systems." Bruce carefully opened his sketchpad to find some of the preliminary drawings he'd done of the creature. "They're rough sketches, but ya get the idea."

She placed a finger on the edge of the paper and tilted it toward the firelight to get a better look. They were character sketches, parts of a face, hair, different scale patterns for the tail, and body shape outlines.

Elodie frowned. "Maybe I still need sleep, but what I'm getting is you drew something to attack me? Why?"

"That was not my intention. I sometimes paint

the motel room walls to mess with my sister and because I find the cream-on-blah typical motel décor to be boring. I wanted to turn it into a theme hotel, each room with a different vibe— 1950s Vegas, so-called mythical creatures, a Cupid room—ya know, things that poke fun at the banality of actual motel life. Like the Clown Motel in Nevada."

"That could be cool," Elodie acknowledged, though she didn't sound too enthused as she stared at the drawings. "But I don't get it. A snake bit me. Not this Echidna-thing-person-creature-animal. Person? I don't know what to call her. Trust me. I would remember if a giant snake lady attacked."

Bruce reached for her hand that held the page toward the light. He wanted to touch her again, to feel that surge of awareness that happened the first time they made contact. Furthermore, his nerves responded, and he felt the tingle work its way along his finger and up his arm. It flooded him like pure desire, causing his body to stir in ways that weren't appropriate to the conversation. He forced himself to pull away.

"My family has been trying to set me up on dates," Bruce said.

"So I've heard."

"Only some of them are using it as an excuse to prank me."

"Ok."

"It's hard to explain."

"Try. It's kind of important for me to understand. I want to know everything."

Bruce nodded. He started to reach for her again but held back. He forced his mind to concentrate. "Raibeart and I enchanted some of my paint supplies so Maura couldn't easily clean it off the walls. It was a game. I'd paint something fun, and she'd come in and magickally scrub it away in seconds. So we made it so that the paint couldn't be magickally removed. That was all well and good. And hilarious."

"Ok." She nodded, urging him to go on.

"Then someone enchanted my paint a second time, and it summoned Echidna off the wall into the hotel room to attack me. It could have been Maura, though, by her reaction, she wasn't too happy with the paint mess Echidna left behind or the fact the room couldn't be used for guests. Still, it would have been poetic for her to do it."

Elodie stared as if willing him to get to the point. The trouble was that Bruce was having difficulty keeping his thoughts together when all he could think about was reaching forward and seeing if the soft skin of her neck would give his hand the same enthusiastic reaction.

"Or it could have been Raibeart. It was his turn to set me up. Or Euann, Or Erik. Or Iain. Really any of my cousins." Bruce sighed. He felt like he wasn't giving her all the facts she needed. "We have this family joke book where we keep score of pranks and whom we have to pay back for, say, that time in the 1800s when I glamoured all of Iain's clothes to look like a peasant woman to other people. Or how my Aunt Margareta moves important objects around to mess with my ma, who's very particular about where things go. Or when Erik was dosed with a love potion spell that made him dance and sing—*rather badly*—in front of the house of the woman he liked. There's a video. It's horrifying and hilarious at the same time. Or when Euann enchanted his sister's date to make him think she had leprosy when he went to kiss her goodnight."

Elodie pressed her lips together, and a tiny snort of a laugh escaped her. "That's awful."

"It was hilarious," Bruce corrected.

"So someone pranked you by enchanting your enchanted paint a second time which brought your painting to life," Elodie prodded.

Bruce nodded. "Aye."

"I'm following. Go on."

"After I managed to squish her back onto the wall, the painting had changed. There were these snake figures going toward the impression of a woman."

"Me?"

"Must have been. It was abstract. I couldn't see your face, just an impression. I didn't think anything of it." His eyes went to the firelight dancing on her cheek, illuminating the shadows of her hair ever so slightly. He wanted to freeze the moment and try to capture it, even as he knew no piece of art would ever do her justice, for she was living art.

"And that's why a snake bit me." She looked as if she believed him, but also that she didn't know if she should.

Bruce nodded. "Turn the page."

She did, dropping Echidna out of view and replacing her with half-sketches of a broken-down car with a flat tire.

Elodie frowned. "My flat when I got out of the hospital? I hadn't even chalked that up to a magickal attack."

"A lot of these are just room ideas. Random thoughts. I was playing with the concept of all the things ya didn't want to happen on a road trip," he said.

She turned another page. The drawing of a beach scene had been scratched out.

"There I was playing juxtaposing that with the whole iconic Americana road-tripping dream," he explained. "It was too *meh*, so I blotted it out."

"Sand." She lightly hovered her hand over the area of the beach that was still showing. Part of a hand poked out of the mess. "You scribbled over the scene, and I was buried in sand in my car."

"Not on purpose. I swear. I didn't know."

Elodie thought for a moment before nodding. "I believe you, Bruce. I saw you outside the motel window talking on your phone. You were drawing figures in the dust with your finger. You swiped it, and I ended up coming to in television land."

"I heard ya fall. Ya were unconscious, so I called for help. My ma and Aunt Margareta came. Ya freaked out, rightly so, and when ya started screaming and tried to run, they petrified ya like I did Euann downstairs. It was to protect ya. When I was waiting for ya to thaw, I started watching television and sketching what was showing." Bruce turned the pages. "Zombies. Commercials. When I realized the woman petrified next to me was trapped inside the television I was watching, I started trying to get ya out. I threw everything I knew at it. Finally, it worked. Ya ended up here."

She looked at the doodles.

He turned the page again to show her the diner. The paper inside the chalkboard menu board on the wall looked like it had been erased multiple times. The words *"Change channel?"* were still written.

"This is how you communicated with me." She nodded. "So that's the how."

"It's my best guess as to what happened," he said.

"I don't get the why me." Elodie kept turning the pages until she got to the sketch of her sleeping. Her eyes darted up to meet his.

"Maybe the magick knew I'd like ya." He smiled and gently closed the pad before returning it to the mantel.

Elodie stretched out on the bed before curling her legs into her chest. She stayed in a ball as she watched him. "Is it over now?"

He wanted to erase the fear he saw in her eyes. He hated that he and his family had something to do with it. That their stupid pranks had somehow spilled onto her and caused her pain was almost too unbearable to think about.

Bruce wanted nothing more than to make that up to her. He wanted to protect her. He wanted to keep her safe.

Beyond that, he wanted to touch her. His hands ached for contact. One small brush of skin, and he was smitten. His magick swirled inside of him, begging to be let free. He felt his body trying to pull energy from the surrounding forest outside the house. It was almost beyond his control.

"Why are you looking at me like that?" She whispered. "Is something happening now? Is something wrong?"

"I can't help myself. I feel myself drawn to ya, love." Bruce held out his hand, palm forward and fingers up. "When we touch, I feel it like I've never felt anything before. Like fire and ice warring inside of me. Even now, my magick is churning."

Elodie lifted her hand and slowly pressed it against his. "I feel what you mean."

The connection joining them grew stronger. The blue threads of his magick escaped his hand to wind around her as if it recognized her and wanted to be a part of her. That desire turned to liquid hot lust. His cock stirred, demanding attention. No, it was more than that. It demanded to be put in charge of the situation.

Bruce fought the urge to let it call the shots. He was not some mindless animal that had to give in to his primal needs. Unfortunately, the rest of his body did not agree with his brain. He found himself twining his fingers into hers, holding her palm to him as he lay beside her on the bed.

Elodie's breathing deepened, and he felt the

softness of it against his cheek. It only added fuel to his emotions. Her eyes moved his mouth as if inviting him forward.

How could he resist?

How could he deny her?

"We just met," she whispered, as of trying not to break the spell, even as she gave a weak protest of what was about to happen. "This is crazy, right?"

"I'm not sure I'm the best person to answer that. All I can think about is kissing ya, touching ya." As if to prove his point, Bruce let go of her fingers and reached for her cheek. It was softer than he had imagined. His magick surged further, begging him to be freed.

Elodie inched closer. Despite her words, she did not stop what was happening between them.

"If ya tell me to go, I will go," Bruce said. "I would never force ya to do something you're unsure of. I know what I want, but that doesn't mean ya have to want it too."

"I'm not sure I'm thinking with a logical brain right now. I know what I should say. I know what the polite ladylike thing to do is. I know that I'm supposed to act coy or hard to get. I know that I'm supposed to make you work for it. But that's not what I want. That's not what I feel. I want to keep touching you." Elodie took a shaky, deep breath. "I feel safe with you, Bruce. When I saw you write that first word in the diner, something inside me told me I could trust you even inside that magical craziness. Even though I didn't know who you were or what was happening, even with fear, it was like a lifeline. No, it was more than that. It was fate."

"Please don't start acting coy." He leaned closer, intent on kissing her. "I find everything about ya refreshing. There are no games in ya, no pretension."

Elodie cut off the rest of what he was going to say by pressing her mouth to his. Magick wound around them like a cocoon. Bruce couldn't control it. Not that he wanted to.

She moaned softly, not demanding but also not shying away from the building passion. Her body slid up against his, the entire length of it pressing into him, cushioned by the robe. The blue light of magick warred with the orange of the firelight.

His hand found its way into her robe, parting the material so that he had access to her. She was naked and more perfect than he had imagined. Heat radiated off, her drawing him closer. He caught her light scent, a sweet mixture of flowers. Everything about her only added fuel to his flame. Bruce wanted to bury his body inside of hers.

If this was only a spell, he never wanted it to break.

Elodie deepened the kiss. Her lips parted, and she slid her tongue along the seam of his mouth, urging him to open to her. He did not take much prodding. As their tongues met and danced with growing passion, Bruce felt as if his body would explode.

His fingers explored beneath the robe, gliding down her neck between the valley of her breasts, along her stomach, and between the apex of her thighs. A shiver worked over him, and his breath caught as he felt the moisture between her legs, a most welcoming discovery.

He parted the slick folds of her sex to find the treasure buried within. She moaned in favor of what he was doing, encouraging him with the flex of her hips. His fingers slid deeper, and he felt her responding, her body trembling and her breath catching. He let his magick reach inside, her giving her pleasure.

Her lips pulled away from him as she gasped for breath. He took advantage of the neck offered to him, kissing and licking his way down her throat to devour a ripe breast.

Elodie tugged at his shirt as her foot worked along the edge of his jeans. Not wanting to pull away, he used his magick to undress. His clothes melted off him and slithered onto the floor. She gave a small laugh of surprise but eagerly followed his lead and began exploring him as he did her. Her fingers moved over his chest and back. She pulled at his shoulders as if to burrow inside his chest. Her stomach bumped his arousal.

It was more than he could bear. He rolled on top of her. Her body sank into the mattress as he maneuvered between her thighs. Her gaze met his, and she nodded. Her eyes begged him to continue.

"I don't know what I did to deserve this moment, but I hope I do it again." Bruce cupped her cheek and kissed her. She stirred against him. The subtle movements of her body combined with his magick. Their kiss deepened.

Her hands slid down his back to his ass. She pulled him into her. The length of his arousal brushed along her thigh. She wiggled beneath him.

She stiffened before he entered her, and she pushed on his shoulder. "Protection? Condom?"

"Magick," he answered.

Elodie took him at his word. She arched her hips, accepting him into her body.

Bruce let her have control. He'd give her anything she wanted. His magick poured into her, deepening their connection. Her heart beat in time with his. Their breathing matched. Their eyes locked and held. Their bodies met in time, thrust for thrust.

If anything, living for centuries had given him many experiences. This was by far the best one. Instinct told him he knew her, that time was nothing more than a construct with no real meaning. Two seconds, two days, two centuries, it wouldn't matter. There was a strand sewing them together, an invisible and indestructible thing that could not be severed.

Bruce had never expected to feel this way. He never expected to be swept off his feet by the mere sound of a woman's voice. He knew that all his cousins and siblings had found love in Green Vallis, Wisconsin, and that they believed it to be some kind of special place. Maybe they were right. He felt the ley lines beneath the town, a powerful convergence of magick that amplified their powers. It made the place special. It acted like a beacon the supernatural kind was drawn to.

"What is it?" she asked.

Bruce realized he'd slowed his thrusts. "You're amazing."

She smiled at him, an infectious humor-filled look that had him grinning like a fool. She gripped his ass and thrust him forward.

Energy pulsed and vibrated out of his hands

to add to her pleasure. Her eyes closed, and her head pressed back into the pillow. Her breath caught in short, audible gasps of ecstasy.

Elodie jerked in release, trembling as her climax ripped through her. It shot his magick back at him, intensifying his pleasure. His climax joined hers. He groaned, unable to stop the loud noise from escaping his throat.

He remained frozen for a long moment, too afraid to move lest he shatter the feeling.

Elodie's hands fell to her side, releasing him.

His heart beat so fast and hard that it drummed in his ears. His insides felt as if they melted, and he was sure that if he tried to stand, he would puddle uselessly onto the floor.

Bruce rolled beside her and wrapped his hand over her naked hip to keep her near. She bit her lip, and her eyes traveled over the ceiling.

"What are ya thinking?" He caressed her cheek, turning her gaze to his.

"Eighteen."

He gave a quizzical laugh. "Eighteen?"

Her eyes searched him just as she had the ceiling. "You said the 1800s before. And when you were on the phone at the motel, you said something about being four hundred years old. I thought it was a joke at the time, but you said your cousins pulled a prank in the 1800s."

"And...?" he prompted.

"You're old, like really old. I'm not sure how I feel about that. I mean, I'm thirty, which I was feeling sorry for myself about, even though I know it's not *that* old." She shrugged. "I just never thought I'd date a man who was old enough to be the best friend of my great-great-great-great-great—"

"All right, I think ya made your point." He tried to kiss her even as she kept talking.

"—great, great—"

He placed his hand over her mouth to stop her.

She added one last muffled, "—*great...*"

"Are ya done?" He waited a few seconds before he removed his hand.

"Grandpa," she finished with a smirk.

"I have a few thoughts about that." He arched a brow and tried to sound firm. He tapped the tip of her nose with his finger. "First, I like to think of it as experienced, not old. Two, thirty is young. All the guys at the Old Man Club will be so jealous when I show them pictures of my trophy lady."

"Oh, really," she laughed.

"Third, I think it's adorable that ya slipped in the fact ya wanted to date me." He turned with her as he rolled onto his back and kept her next to him. "Aye, love, I'll be your boyfriend. We can go steady. I'll carry your books, and ya can wear my pin. Maybe we can go to the sock hop if you're lucky."

"Aw," she teased. "You know, I feel kind of bad."

"Why?"

"All those blind dates you're going to have to cancel. Your ma will be so disappointed," Elodie snuggled against him, getting comfortable.

"If you're so worried about my ma, just tell her that ya plan on giving her thirty grandchildren. That will perk her right up."

Elodie gave a soft cough of surprise. "You want *thirty* kids?"

"Why not. As ya implied, I'm old-fashioned. You're the one who'll be raising them. I'll come home from the bar long enough to be the fun dad."

Elodie punched him lightly in the side and laughed. "That's not even funny."

"It's a little funny," he disagreed. Happiness filled him at how easy it was to be with her.

"Fine. Maybe a little." Elodie gave a long sigh and closed her eyes. She draped her arm over his stomach. "I'm exhausted. I feel like I ran three marathons."

"Then rest." Bruce kissed her forehead. "There is nowhere else we have to be."

Her arm tightened over him. "Don't leave. I don't want to be alone."

He moved his lips to her temple and kissed her again. "I'm here."

She mumbled something but didn't open her eyes as she fell asleep. He watched her for a long time until his eyes could no longer remain open.

Chapter Nine

Elodie woke up confused and disorientated. Her head felt heavy as she tried to get the willpower to crawl out of bed. Blankets tangled her limbs, holding her down like silky prison guards. It had been a long time since she'd slept so deeply that she couldn't remember her dreams.

Blue light surrounded her, like sunlight coming through the surface of a swimming pool, only she wasn't underwater. She watched it dance over her head, blocking the ceiling.

Magick.

Elodie automatically reached for Bruce. "Are you—?"

He wasn't next to her.

"Bruce?" she called, rolling to look toward the

bathroom. Through the blue lights surrounding the bed like a shield, she saw the toilet and sink through the open door. He wasn't in there.

Elodie pushed up from the mattress in alarm. Her heart leaped in her chest, giving her a nauseated feeling in her stomach. What now?

"Bru...?" She let the word die on her lips as she saw a piece of paper lying on the bed where he should have been.

Picking up the note, she read, *"You're safe. My magick will protect you. I'm finding out who did this to you so we can stop it. Breakfast downstairs when you're ready. Sorry in advance about my family. They mean well."*

Next to the words was a drawing of her sleeping with the protective magick all around her. Elodie ran her hand along the barrier and felt the tingling of Bruce's presence.

"Breakfast?" She looked toward the window. Light edged the dark curtain, but it was impossible to tell time by it, only that it wasn't the middle of the night. The fireplace had burned out. Had she slept a full day or only a few hours?

Clothes were neatly folded at the end of the bed. She didn't stop to consider who they belonged to as she pulled on a 1980s rock band t-shirt and gray leggings. She didn't bother getting out of bed as she stood on the mattress to pull the leggings into place. They weren't hers, but they fit well enough. The wool socks definitely belonged to a man...or a woman with large feet. She supposed she shouldn't presume.

She dropped down on the mattress before bouncing her way off the bed.

Elodie expected the magick to burst like a bubble when she hopped through. Instead, the barrier came with her, surrounding her.

"I'm in a human hamster ball." Elodie laughed at the notion. If she stretched her arms wide and leaned a little, she could touch the sides. She couldn't help but watch the circular barrier as she walked toward the bathroom door. The glow bent into the shape of the frame as she went through.

After checking herself in the mirror to ensure she was more presentable than the last time she'd been downstairs, Elodie left the room and walked down the hall. She watched the glowing magick morph around objects. She tried bumping against the sharp edge of a narrow table in the hallway only to be softly pushed back unharmed.

Elodie went to the railing overlooking the foyer. Her glowing ball went with her, hanging over the edge. A passing thought urged her to see if she could jump down safely, wondering if she would bounce around like the inside of a ball. She didn't listen to it. The marble looked way too hard of a landing.

Silence rose from below.

Elodie thought about leaving, of trying to find the motel and her own clothes. She doubted a woman walking down the street in a magick ball would go unnoticed.

She made her way down the stairs, watching the dining room door for movement. Euann's frozen arm was gone.

"Hello?" she called. "Bruce, are you down here?"

Silence.

Elodie frowned. Actually, it was too quiet. She heard her own voice but no ambient noises like birds chirping outside or an air conditioner running.

"Hello?"

She went to the dining room and looked in. The long table had been pre-set with elegant place settings, and the chairs were tucked into position. It looked ready for a magazine photoshoot. A platter of pastries was placed in the middle, the tower of baked goods so perfect it seemed wrong to take one.

Seeing another doorway, she crossed toward a kitchen. Her magickal hamster ball morphed around the chairs as she passed. "Is anyone home?"

Still nothing. The kitchen was empty.

Elodie frowned, starting to get nervous. Surely she should hear something outside of her ball. She hoped this wasn't another trick or prank.

"Bruce?"

She crossed past the kitchen and found a home office library. The old books were arranged in such a way that looked more form than function.

"Why did ya even mention it to her?" a woman demanded.

Elodie followed the voice.

"She asked," another answered. "Would ya lie to Muma Pădurii if she asked ya a question point blank? I think not."

She found a backdoor leading to a garden. The two women from the motel sat on a bench watching the trees. They were angled toward each other with their backs toward the house.

"Was she upset?" Margareta turned her head to study Cait.

"She sent a white bird into the house," Cait answered.

Margareta nodded. "Oh, yeah, she's mad."

"Bruce told me he likes this Elodie girl." Cait looked up at the second story as if staring at the guest room window. "We can't force him to take Ullah out on a date to appease the old crone."

"Keep calling her an old crone. Flattery will get ya everywhere." Margareta sounded serious. "Maybe we call Raibeart's boys for a favor? They are family. Technically."

"If ya can find them," Cait said. "Donovan and Gregory haven't exactly been family joiners."

"Do ya expect anything else? Raised by an evil witch is worse than feral. Niall might know where they're at." Margareta stood and held out her hand. "Shh."

"What is it?" Cait joined her. They both looked toward Elodie.

"Uh, hi. I didn't mean to interrupt. I was looking for Bruce," Elodie said.

"Someone is watching us," Margareta stated, concerned.

"Aye. I feel it," Cait answered.

"Yeah, hello, I was looking for—" Elodie stepped into the garden and waved.

"Ya think Muma Pădurii sent another omen warning?" Cait asked.

"We can't be too sure." Margareta strode toward the door. "I'll have Euann renew all the protection spells. Ya should call Maura and tell her to keep an eye on baby Tina. I'll tell Kenneth to watch Jewel, though may the gods help anyone who tries to hurt a phoenix."

"Can't you see me?" Elodie asked as Margareta walked right by her. The woman didn't break stride.

Cait followed Margareta. She held out her hand, and a cellphone materialized in it.

Elodie could only watch. She didn't know what it meant that magickal people couldn't see the magick surrounding her.

Elodie stared at the forest beyond the manicured garden. Unlike inside the house, outside she could hear the sound the wind made through the trees. Instead of following Cait and Margareta, she walked around the side of the house to the front drive. It didn't feel right being inside somebody's home when they didn't know she was there.

Where was Bruce? She really wanted to see him.

The trees curled around the side of the property so that the house and unattached garage were nestled within. Cars were still parked in the drive but had moved from where they were previously. Like inside the home, everything outside was well maintained. Not that she expected anything different.

The jagged stones did not hurt her feet when she stepped on the cobblestone driveway. The magick protected not only her but the bottom of her wool socks. She walked into the yard and turned to look up at the house. She searched the windows to see if anybody was watching her through the glass.

The sound of a car drew her attention around. A green Pontiac GTO sped toward her. Elodie raised her hands to wave. The driver didn't slow, didn't swerve. She dove to the side to avoid being hit. The magick cushion stopped her from landing hard. She scrambled to her feet and turned toward the taillights as the car stopped in front of the house. Two men in kilts got out and started to walk inside. She recognized Euann.

Elodie hurried after them. "Excuse me! Euann, hello? I'm looking for…"

They kept walking. The man she didn't know scratched his ass, and the gesture lifted his kilt to give her a flash.

Elodie averted her eyes. It felt wrong checking out another man after her night with Bruce. "Euann, can you see me?"

An eerie feeling washed over her, followed by a sense of fear. What if Bruce hadn't left that note? What if this was another wayward spell? What if she were invisible?

"I'm the invisible woman in a hamster ball,"

she muttered. "And this isn't even the strangest thing to happen this week."

Elodie knew what it felt like to be alone, even when standing in a crowded room, or never to be heard, even when she raised her voice. What if this ghostlike state was permanent?

There was so much about the magickal world she didn't understand. What little she could assume came from fiction movies and books. But how much of that was real, and how much was a writer's imagination?

Elodie glanced at the house and then down the driveway, indecisive about where she should go. Finally, she hurried to follow the men inside. Being where she last saw Bruce seemed like the best decision.

One of the men waved his hand, and the door started to close on her only to bounce off the protective bubble. "Och, we have ghosts again."

"Your magick is as hungover as ya, Iain," Euann teased. He mimicked the first one's gesture. Elodie hopped out of the way so she wouldn't stop the door from closing again. "See. Magick so simple even baby Tina could do it."

Iain grumbled in another language. He again scratched his backside.

Euann laughed. "Don't let ma hear ya talking like that, Uncle Chicken."

"Any idea why they sent for us?" Iain asked. He stopped in the dining room doorway and looked inside.

"Bruce brought home a lassie," Euann said.

"To this house?" Iain asked in surprise. "He might as well tell Aunt Cait he's getting married. I almost feel sorry for her. Cait will be feeding her fertility potions if she's not careful."

"She's not the only one. Ma tried giving Cora something she called a mere trinket. Of course, she waited until I was out of town to do it. It turns out the damned thing was bartered from a sea witch to induce motherly cravings."

"What did ya do with it?" Iain asked, again reaching for his ass.

"Returned it to the sea," he said.

"When did ya go to the sea?" Iain turned from the dining room to look along the upper level.

"Flushed it down the library toilet," Euann amended. "I don't want my wife giving birth to mermen. It's bad enough that I shift into a fox, and ya are a chicken. Can ya imagine a fish for a son?"

"Bird," Iain stated, rubbing a temple. "You're the chicken."

"Ya are very grumpy this morning." Euann laughed. "I told ya not to try to keep up with Raibeart last night."

Iain grumbled again.

"Stop showing me the full monty," Euann protested, lifting his hand to block Iain from view. "What's wrong with your arse?"

Elodie couldn't help herself. She turned to look as Iain lifted his kilt.

"Raibeart invited me on one of his runs," Iain said. "I think someone shot magick at us in the forest."

Elodie flinched to see the red splotches. "Oh, ow, that's one place you do *not* want poison ivy."

"Och!" Euann recoiled, lifting both hands. Yellow magick shot from his fingers to zap Iain.

Elodie gasped and hopped back even though it didn't come close to hitting her.

Iain froze with his kilt lifted and his ass hanging out for all to see.

"Who is yelling?" Margareta's voice carried from beyond the dining room. She hurried toward them. "Iain —*dammit.*"

Euann looked around the mostly empty foyer and looked as if he might try to make a run for it. He was too late.

Margareta appeared next to the Iain statue. "Euann MacGregor! What have we told ya about freezing your brothers? I swear it's like all of ya are two hundred years old again, running around and shooting magick without a care in the world."

"Like you and Cait froze me at the motel?" Elodie muttered.

The woman's eyes turned in her direction but didn't focus on her.

"Ma, listen, I did it for his own good. He's got a red arse," Euann motioned toward Iain's backside. "Think of the furniture."

Margareta came around to look for herself. She gave a pointedly loud sigh. "Well, if ya could keep your kilts on, maybe ya wouldn't have this problem."

"Iain's the one who went running about with Raibeart, Ma. I didn't," Euann said.

"Stop kissing up," Margareta stated, though her lips twitched up at the corner in a small smile. She gave a slight wave to encompass Iain. "I'll have Cait look at this."

"I think everyone is going to be looking at this." Euann snickered but then covered his mouth and instantly looked apologetic.

"Ya could have at least petrified him away from the front door," Margareta said.

"Why am I here, Ma?"

"We need ya to renew the protection spells," Margareta ordered. "All of them. Start with the house, then move back to the gardens, then the woods. And turn on those spy viewers."

"Video cameras," he stated.

"Aye, those. Get on it."

"But I just did the protection spells a few months ago," Euann protested. "It'll take all day to redo all of them. Cora wanted me to take her out to dinner tonight."

"Well, then ya better make sure ya do it correctly this time. A white bird got into the house today, and I don't think that's the last unexpected visitor." Margareta again glanced in her direction but didn't detect her. "And tell Cora she's coming here for dinner tonight. Problem solved."

Elodie waved her hands and wished the woman could see her.

"White bird? Ya are making me redo the spells because of a lost bird," Euann frowned.

Margareta arched a brow. "I was going to make Iain help, but…"

"Fine!" Euann kicked his heel a little as he went to the stairs.

Margareta watched her son until he was gone. Her eye stayed on the stairs as she said, "I don't know what ya want, but ya will not find it here."

"I want…" Elodie hesitated. She wasn't sure how to finish the statement.

I want to go home?

I want to be seen?

I want to know magick doesn't exist again?

I don't want to be here.

"I want Bruce," she whispered. "Where is he?"

"Whoever ya are, this is no place for ghosts." Margareta strode from the foyer, moving with purpose.

Elodie hugged her arms around her waist as she stared at Iain's frozen form. She thought of all the times she'd wished something extraordinary would happen to her, how she planned to travel and find herself, and prayed it would be amazing. She should have been more specific in her daydreams.

Elodie didn't understand this world of magick. She didn't know how to communicate or make it stop. She couldn't…

Communicate!

Elodie looked around the foyer. The chalkboard in the diner had allowed her to speak to Bruce. All she had to do was find another method to let him know she needed help.

She moved around Iain, pausing briefly to study his face as she looked for signs of life. He was literally like a statue. Elodie moved past him to the dining room. Seeing the platter of baked goods, she reached across the table and moved it closer. She automatically shoved a donut in her mouth and held it as she began arranging the rest of them on the wood to spell, "*Help*."

She paced back and forth between the two doorways, eager for someone to appear to answer her sense of urgency. When no one did, she slowly took a seat to wait. She pulled the donut from her mouth and began to chew. It shouldn't be long now.

Chapter Ten

Awareness came long before Bruce could move his body. He stared angrily at the back interior of the Macgregor garage. Spiders had called a long beam home. Their webs drifted down, caked with dirt to make them more visible. He could guess it had been hours by the way the light moved through a window.

It had not been his intention to abandon Elodie for so long. He had only meant to question which of his family members had cast the misfired spell so he could make sure they reversed it. None of them would have intentionally harmed her in their pursuit to mess with him.

At least he knew she was safe inside the family home. There was no securer place in all of the

United States. Bruce had cast the strongest protection spell his magick could summon.

With frozen limbs, he had no choice but to wait the petrifying spell out as his mind fixated on Elodie. In the span of his centuries, the moments with her were fleeting and few, but they meant more to him than a million warlock lifetimes. What was time anyway, but some construct to be followed and tallied and watched as it slipped away? Not every minute was equal. Not every second should be counted.

For once, he was interested in savoring something more than was written in a novel or painted on the wall. He wanted to live in that perfect moment when her eyes met his in passion for the first time, in a bed, clinging together under the scent of sweat and the music of heavy breathing.

Love hardly seemed the word for his emotions. It was too small, too overused, and given to too many activities. How could he say his feelings for Elodie matched what men in this state said about football and beer? Or how some women felt about a giant walk-in closet filled with shoes?

His mind became obsessed, trying to come up with the perfect word. Forever? Infinity? Bonded? Heart-struck?

Nothing worked.

He felt the forest outside, stretching for undisturbed acres. His magick tried to wake up and call the energy from the trees so he could break free faster, but that is not how this spell worked.

As much as he hated being trapped, he was grateful that it was him and not Elodie. At least he had the boring wall and spiders. He couldn't imagine how frightened she had been trapped inside television programming without the magick to defend herself.

Feeling began to return like an itch he was unable to reach. It progressed like slow torture over his skin. Bruce counted the seconds, brought back to the concept of time. A second with Elodie was too short. A second without her felt like hours.

His finger twitched, and he focused on moving his hand. Then, as suddenly as it struck, the spell ended. His body dropped forward like dead weight before he caught himself. Stiff muscles made his gait awkward, but he didn't care as he limp-ran out of the garage.

As he suspected, too much time had passed. One of Euann's new toys was parked in the drive. He touched the hood, feeling it was cool. Bruce had not heard the Pontiac pull up, so it must have happened when the spell had been the strongest.

The mansion was unusually quiet, mainly due to most of the extended family having moved out.

Living together had been fine when his relatives were adult bachelors willing to be cared for by their mothers. Once they married, the wives hadn't been too hip to the lack of privacy that multi-generational living provided.

Bruce continued past the cars toward the front steps. The air seemed particularly thick with magickal residue, as if someone had called great power from the forest. He frowned in concern. Bruce could think of very few reasons to expend that much energy and they weren't currently locked in a magickal war.

The house vibrated when he touched the door handle to open it. Inside, the oppressive feeling of magick became worse, like humidity hanging thick in the air. Iain's frozen form greeted him. His cousin had been mid-moon, his kilt lifted.

Bruce grimaced and ignored it as he rushed upstairs to search for Elodie. She wasn't in the bedroom, but the sketchpad rested on the bed. He saw the drawing he'd left for her showing on top. He picked up the pad and held it to his chest. If it were enchanted, he'd have his mother lock it in the family vault for safekeeping.

Leaving the bedroom, he ran along the hall and took the stairs two at a time. His feet echoed loudly, and he half expected one of the matriarchal elders to scold him for the noise.

"Help myself? Don't mind if I do." Raibeart's voice came from the dining room.

Bruce hurried around Iain to find Raibeart playing with a tray of pastries on the dining room table. His uncle wore a green fishnet tank top, yellow crocheted short pants, and a beret.

"Have ya seen Elodie?" Bruce asked.

"Aye," Raibeart pulled back from the table, holding a Danish. "Lovely little lassie. Don't know what she sees in ya, but there is no accounting for taste."

Bruce glanced down to see Raibeart had written the word "*Hell*" on the tabletop. He ignored his uncle's eccentricities, dismissing the food tasting as another way for Raibeart to irritate Cait.

"Where is she?" Bruce demanded, keeping the sketchpad close.

"Where is who?" Raibeart set the Danish down with a bite missing and took a donut instead.

"Elodie," Bruce insisted. He felt a tickle along his cheek and rubbed it.

"How should I know?" Raibeart started to set down a donut missing a bite when he paused to give Bruce a pitied look. "Ah, I'm sorry, laddie. Ya ran her off already? Did ya remember to tell her she was sparkly like the stars? Or that her breasts were ripe melons?"

"Don't talk about her breasts," Bruce warned.

"Och, not me. Ya, laddie, *ya*! The ladies like to be told romantical things like that. Sweeps them off their feet."

"I thought ya said ya saw her," Bruce insisted. A chill of cold air drifted over him. He glanced around, not sensing the source. "Where is she?"

"Aye, yesterday. Ya saw her too." Raibeart shook his head and put down his used donut only to take another. The man looked intent on sampling each one. "Ya should ask her to marry ya. Ladies like that too. Then ya will always know where she is, and ya won't have to ask me."

Raibeart had spent the last few centuries proposing to every woman he met. Surprisingly, the warlock had found one to say yes.

Bruce placed his hand over his uncle's to stop his progress. "Uncle Raibeart, this is important. Did ya enchant my paint supplies at the motel again?"

"Why would I do that?" Raibeart bit the top of a muffin and set it back down. He waved his hand as if shooing a fly, even though Bruce didn't see one.

"Because ya thought it funny?" Bruce put his

hand on Raibeart's to stop him from picking up another baked good.

"Oh, then, aye, maybe." Raibeart nodded and slapped Bruce's hand away to continue his strange mission. "Funny sounds like me. I'm hilarious."

"I need to know exactly what ya did to manifest Echidna?"

Raibeart wrinkled his nose and frowned. "Why would I manifest Echidna? I lost a bet and still owe her twenty thousand drachmas."

"That's like sixty bucks US," Bruce countered.

"Aye, but she wants it in silver. I'd have to rob an Ancient Greece exhibit, and your ma ordered no more breaking into museums." Raibeart gave a slight shiver of disgust. "Echidna offered to work it out in trade, but I'm a married man now."

"Plus, she's half snake," Bruce said. Another chill ran up his arm.

"Well, aye, that too." Raibeart bit another donut and waved Bruce to leave him alone. "Go hassle your da. I already told ya all of my advice Ask Elodie to marry ya and tell her she looks like the stars. And don't talk about Echidna. Ladies don't like it when ya talk about manifesting other women on your dates. Oh, and don't take drinks from witches trying to steal your magick. That's one roofie ya will live to regret. Trust me."

Whatever that meant.

Bruce sighed in frustration, though he wasn't shocked at Raibeart's lack of help. "Find me if ya see her again."

"Who? Echidna?"

"Elodie!"

"No need to shout," Raibeart scolded.

Bruce left the dining room and hurried past the kitchen and library. Many of the elders lived in the first-level wing beyond.

"Ma!" Bruce called.

One of the bedroom doors opened, and his father peeked out into the hall. Murdoch MacGregor had the dark hair and proud features that ran strong in the family genetics. People said Bruce and his twin favored their father.

"Da, you're back." He hugged his father.

"My flight got in this morning." Murdoch grinned. "Your ma tells me ya brought a lady home. Must be serious if ya risked your ma meeting her."

"Maybe I just wanted the blind dates to stop," Bruce answered.

Murdoch shrugged. "Don't look at me. It was not my idea. I was not at that family meeting."

"There was a family meeting?" Bruce sighed. Of course, there had been a family meeting. He could see them all throwing out suggestions at his ma's behest. "Any chance ya know where the lady is?"

Murdoch laughed. "Has ya running around already, does she? Get used to it, son. My Cait has had me chasing after her for the last five hundred years. No better thing in the world than to love a woman. Let yourself fall into it and give her whatever she desires. Even when she's not, she's right."

Bruce's father was a hopeless romantic and entirely in love with his wife. Bruce and Rory used to joke that their ma had put a romantically whipped spell over their da. It almost appeared physically painful sometimes for Murdoch to be away from her.

His father didn't care what anyone else said or how he was teased. Bruce was beginning to understand why.

"The first moment I saw your ma, everything inside me lined up." Murdoch clapped his son's shoulder and motioned for him to return to the library.

"Do ya know where Ma is? I need to talk to her." Bruce held the sketchpad against his chest.

"Your ma and Margareta are out back supervising Euann. He's renewing the protection spells. Something about ghosts and white birds."

Raibeart appeared holding a donut. "We have

a poltergeist. If Cait asks, it took bites out of all the donuts."

"That was ya," Bruce drawled.

"Not if Cait asks," Raibeart answered, sauntering past to go to his bedroom. He twirled the donut around on his index finger as he opened the door, saying, "Katherine, no need to get dressed. I made ya breakfast in bed."

Bruce instantly turned in the other direction to go outside. No part of him wanted to overhear anything happening in that room.

His da was already at the back garden door when Bruce reached the library.

"Let me know if ya see her," Bruce called after his father.

"Aye." Murdoch waved a hand, indicating he'd heard.

Another chill came over him, and Bruce frowned. Maybe they really did have ghosts in the house.

"Elodie?" Bruce asked the empty room. A new ghost that appeared at the same time Elodie disappeared? That couldn't be a coincidence. "Is that ya, love? Can ya hear me? Please try to tell me where ya are."

Chapter Eleven

"Bruce! Bruce!"

Elodie waved her hands to get his attention as she screamed in his face. She'd tried throwing things in his direction, but after she picked up the object and launched it, the thing would reappear in place like she'd done nothing. Her magick bubble protected her from being seen. She could only assume that the donuts hadn't replaced themselves because Raibeart was the one who found them, and he didn't seem phased by her plea for help.

"*Bruce!*" Her voice was getting hoarse from the yelling.

He rubbed his cheek.

Elodie looked at the sketchpad he held. She

slapped her hand against it to make him drop it. His hands dipped a little but not enough to make an impression.

"Dammit, Elodie, where are ya?" He frowned as he looked at the drawing.

She expected him to follow his father outside, but he sat at the desk and pulled out a pencil instead. She stood behind him to watch.

Bruce tapped the pencil several times like a drumstick before writing on the page. "*Elodie?*"

"Yes, I'm here." Elodie touched his hand, feeling him like normal. He didn't appear to feel her in return. She snatched the pencil from him, but he didn't notice. She reached toward the shelf and pulled off books. They fell on the floor by her feet, making loud thuds. She turned for a reaction, and the books replaced themselves as soon as she stepped away from the shelf.

Bruce looked around the room as if expecting something to happen. He reached for the sketchpad, and the pencil reappeared in his hand as if she hadn't touched it. He drew what looked to be the chalkboard in the diner before writing her name on it.

"Answer me, Elodie," he whispered. "Come on, love. Where are ya?"

"I'm here," Elodie pleaded. She put her hands on his face and kissed him. "See me."

"Maybe I need a television." Bruce frowned. He dropped his head into his hands and rubbed his face where she touched him.

Elodie gave up. She dropped onto the floor and sat against a bookcase. She had thought that if she could find Bruce, he'd be able to see her, and her time as a ghost would be over.

"I'm here," she whispered. "Why can't you see that I'm right here?"

ELODIE'S HIPS ached from sitting on the hard floor. Her throat was sore from screaming. Hours had passed. At least, she thought it had to be hours. It felt like an eternity, but she had no real concept of time.

Bruce magickally materialized a television and spent a long time flipping channels and staring at the screen to look for her. Various members of his family passed through, and Bruce stopped to ask them if they knew anything about the spell at the motel. No one copped to it.

At one point, Raibeart streaked past, only to pass a second time in the other direction with more donuts. Bruce barely glanced in the man's direction.

This was a house of insanity.

Elodie laid on her back on the library floor and bent her knees to help take pressure off her hips. Bruce pulled books from the shelf and seemed to be studying them. A few took a wave of magick before he could open them.

"As I was saying before, I don't think my parents will even realize I'm missing. Do you know how sad that is to know no one will even think to look for you? It'll probably be Christmas before they take note, and only then because I don't attend their stupid holiday party." Elodie lifted her head and craned her neck to see his back. "I bet your family would notice if you were gone. They seem close."

"Did ya see who zapped me?" Iain appeared from the kitchen.

"No, but my money is on Euann. He got me earlier in the garage," Bruce said. "Did ya cast any spells on me at the motel? Some enchantment on my artwork to make it come to life? Dating prank? Anything?"

"Your ma wanted a list of names of all the single ladies that Jane and I know. Is that what ya mean?"

Bruce shook his head. "No. I thought a spell had gone awry, but now…"

"What are ya up to?" Iain asked.

"Elodie's missing."

"Euann said ya met someone," Iain acknowledged. "Good for you, cousin."

"I'm trying to find her."

"In a book?" Iain yawned. He scratched his ass. "Please tell me this Elodie is real and not some character ya read. What do they call them? Book girlfriends?"

"She's real," Bruce grumbled, studying the page.

"Wouldn't ya be better off locating someone with a map?"

"I tried that already." Bruce waved his hand, sending the books flying back to the shelf where they belonged. "I was hoping one of those spells would tell me how to find her, but I'm not even sure what kind of magick I'm dealing with."

"Ya look exhausted," Iain stated. "Want to take a break and go get a beer? Talk about it?"

"I'm going to the motel to check. Maura said she'd call if Elodie showed, but she gets busy sometimes." Bruce stood. "Give me your keys. Euann hid my car somewhere. It wasn't in the driveway."

"I don't have them," Iain said. "Hotwire Euann's."

Bruce nodded. Elodie scrambled to her feet to follow him.

"Hey, wait a second. Slow down. Before ya

run all over town searching for someone ya can't find with a simple location spell, tell me what's up. Why did ya ask about art? Do ya think someone cast a spell on your artwork?" Iain stopped Bruce from leaving. "And that somehow Elodie is missing because of it?"

"Aye." Bruce gave a watered-down, quick version of what had been happening.

"Where did ya last see her?" Iain questioned, sounding reasonable against Bruce's panic.

"Uh, I…" He looked upwards. "In bed this morning. I…"

"Did she say anything?" Iain persisted.

"She was sleeping." Bruce went to the sketchpad he'd forgotten on the desk and pointed at it. "I wanted to find out whose stupid prank when awry, so I cast a protection spell and left her there. I thought she would be safe, but now I can't find her and don't know where to look. Everyone swears they weren't messing with me."

"What kind of protection spell?"

Bruce gestured at the pad. "Since my art can hurt her, I figured it could also protect her. I drew my magick protecting her from all harm."

"And she's not Sleeping Beauty-ing on the bed?" Iain looked at the drawing of Elodie sleep-ing. "She's beautiful."

"Aye." Bruce nodded. "She's amazing. When I'm with her, I want to know everything about her all at once, but also nothing so I can spend an eternity discovering her secrets. I don't know how else to explain it."

"Ley lines," Iain nodded in understanding. "I've been trying to tell ya. This place is magickal, so much more than we could ever have anticipated. I felt the exact same way when I met Jane. Maybe all this intrigue you're talking about is merely your magick at work to bring her to ya."

"My magick would not have threatened her life or tried to terrorize her into needing me. I know that is not it." Bruce started to reach for the sketchpad. "I'll try the motel."

Iain put a hand on his arm to stop him as he stared at the sketchpad. He gave a small laugh. "I think I know what ya need to do."

"What? Anything."

"Grab that pencil," Iain instructed. When Bruce obeyed, he said, "Now erase the protection spell."

Bruce looked at the pencil, skeptical.

"Do it," Iain ordered.

Bruce went to the drawing and erased a small piece of circular magick surrounding her picture.

"As I suspected." Iain's eyes met hers, and he

grinned. "I don't suppose this floating head is what you've been looking for?"

"Oh, thank God. You can see me?" Elodie sighed in relief.

Bruce looked at her face before glancing down. "Where is the rest of ya? Are ya harmed? Are ya safe?"

Elodie glanced down, able to see her body. She waved her arms. "I'm here."

"Erase the rest of the circle. Let her out," Iain said before saying to Elodie, "Ya must be Elodie. Lovely to meet ya."

"Thank you," she rushed. "I can't tell you how grateful I am to be seen."

"Was that ya in the foyer with the door?" Iain asked.

"Yes." She nodded. "Sorry. I was trying to find help. I thought I had, but then Raibeart ate my message."

"That jackass," Bruce grumbled, erasing furiously.

"There she is," Iain said.

Bruce dropped the pencil and rushed to Elodie. He held her against him, tight. "I'm sorry. I don't know why I didn't think to erase the spell I cast this morning."

"What's the saying? Ya weren't seeing the trees for the forest," Iain said. "Glad that's solved.

Now, have ya seen Euann? I want to have a wee chat with him about my little bare-arsed statue nap."

"You, uh, have poison ivy on your, ah…" Elodie put forth. "I didn't mean to look, but you should get calamine lotion for the rash, or it will spread and get worse."

"Oh, aye. Thanks. My wife will have something." Iain twisted to check the back of his legs. He glanced at Bruce. "Euann?"

Bruce kept hold of her. "Aye, out back. He's renewing protection spells. They've been at it all day. Ya might let them know we found our ghost, and they can stop. No need to prepare for a magickal war that's not happening."

"Forget that. I'm going to tell him he missed a spot, so he's up all night doing it over." Iain left them alone.

"I'm so sorry, Elodie." Bruce's hands ran up and down her arms before finding their way to cup her face.

"Where did you go this morning?" she asked. "Why did you leave me?"

"I only made it as far as the garage before Euann caught me. He wasn't pleased with my petrifying him for eavesdropping, so he got me back." Bruce's grip tightened. "I'm so sorry. I wasn't supposed to be gone that long."

Elodie wiggled so he'd ease up and she could look at his face.

"Dare I ask how your day was?" he asked.

"When all is said and done, I hope I don't come back as a ghost." Elodie tried to laugh, but the sound was weak. "It was strange overhearing everyone's conversations. I probably heard some things I shouldn't have. It didn't matter what I did. No one could hear me. I even threw books at you while you were at the desk. Nothing. It's a horrible feeling to be invisible."

"What did ya overhear?"

"Your mom and aunt didn't seem pleased that you're dating me. They were discussing you being with someone named Ullah to stop bad omens by someone named…? Honestly, I was so busy trying to get them to see me that I didn't absorb everything they were saying."

Bruce frowned. "Muma Pădurii sent an omen?"

"Bird," Elodie answered. "Is that helpful?"

"Muma Pădurii doesn't leave Romania," Bruce said. "At least, I've never heard of her doing so."

"Iain said ya were done with your project." Cait joined them. "Good to see ya again, Elodie. Will ya be joining us for dinner?"

"I…?" She looked at Bruce for help.

"Aye," Bruce said.

"Ten minutes." Cait swept out of the room as quickly as she arrived.

Elodie didn't think his mother cared for her, and the invitation felt more like an obligation invite than a friendly one. "I don't think that's a good idea. Maybe I should go back to the motel."

"I understand why ya would want to, but I am uncomfortable letting ya out of my sight. Please, stay for dinner so we can let them know what is happening and hopefully put an end to it. I promise, after, if ya still want to go to the motel, I'll take ya." Bruce stroked her cheek. "I don't know what I would have done if I lost ya."

Elodie had been frightened but could find no reason to make him feel worse than he already did. "It's all right. We're here. We're figuring it out. I appreciate your help."

"I am..." Bruce studied her as if struggling with his words. "Fascinated."

"Fascinated?" she repeated, not following.

He nodded. "Aye. Ya fascinate me, Elodie."

Elodie gazed up at him. She thought of all the things he must have seen in his life, magickal things, things beyond her imagination. And he was fascinated by her?

"Did I say something wrong?" He continued

to touch her face as if feeling her cheek required all his attention.

"I don't think anyone has ever called me fascinating before." She reached to feel the texture of his stubbled cheek against her palm. "I don't know that it's a compliment I deserve."

What had she done with her life? This trip was supposed to be her big moment to break free from her family, but that hardly qualified as fascinating.

"It breaks my heart to think that ya can't see it." Bruce leaned forward and kissed her softly. His lips were gentle, sweeping back and forth along hers.

Elodie closed her eyes, enjoying his exploration. The moment hardly seemed real. She felt the kiss throughout her body. All traces of anxiety melted away. "Are you using magick on me?"

"No. Would ya like me to?"

The answer took her by surprise. She opened her eyes, expecting to see the blue swirls coming off his hands to cause the tingling awareness coursing through her. There was only Bruce and his gentle kiss.

"I can think of two things I would like." Elodie dropped her hand onto his chest. "I want to pause all of this magickal curse stuff, take a step back, and find my bearings."

"If I could do that, I would," Bruce said. "And the other thing?"

Elodie leaned into him. "You."

Bruce grinned, looking very much like a kid who'd been given the keys to the candy store. A playful light entered his eyes. "Aye. That ya can have, love."

It wasn't lost on her how life had shifted in such a short time. From being alone praying for a change to being trapped in a magickal world with a man who shot electricity through her with just a look. Would she even want to rewind time and go back to the way things were if that meant she'd be safe again? If the cost of that safety was never having known Bruce?

"What are ya thinking?" He loosened his grip on her.

"That I'm scared because I don't know what is going to happen next. And my heart is beating fast, but I don't know if that's fear or excitement for what may come." She looked past him as a couple of his family members walked through the library. They glanced in Bruce's direction but didn't speak. She lowered her voice to a whisper. "And I don't think your family likes me."

"They don't know ya," Bruce said. "Supernaturals and humans haven't always gotten along well. They're waiting to see what kind of person ya are. They'll come around once they realize the bad omens aren't your fault."

Raibeart and a woman passed by.

"Last one to the table marries a banshee," Raibeart taunted.

"Is he…?" Elodie didn't finish the sentence because it felt too rude.

"Aye, insane," Bruce said. "But he's our insanity, and we love him all the same."

Chapter Twelve

Family dinner did not go well.

Bruce had to stop himself from freezing the entire table out of irritation. For weeks, they'd been setting him up on dates, begging him to settle down, and now that he had met a woman he could consider settling down with, they eyed her suspiciously and made her uncomfortable.

Raibeart sat by his wife, Katherine. They usually only had eyes for each other. Since Katherine had spent centuries as the prisoner of an evil bitch, Bruce could forgive her lack of manners. The effects of living alone for so long had caused her to be somewhat socially awkward during large family gatherings. And this wasn't even the entire family.

Iain brought his wife, Jane. As a natural green

witch and owner of a plant nursery, she concerned herself with the gardens. She spent most of the evening discussing exactly what Euann had done with his protection spells that caused the back shrubbery to look so sickly.

Euann's wife, Cora, seemed irritated with Jane's questioning since the protection spells had taken him away from helping her with a shipment at the library.

Whereas most of the family was busy with their own problems, Margareta and Cait paid too much attention to Elodie. They asked her questions about her family, about her job, about her heritage. Bruce knew they were trying to figure out why she was under magickal attack, but the interview came off rude.

The only friendly face ended up being his father. Murdoch broke in whenever the interrogation became too much, telling a joke or turning the tide of the conversation into something more pleasant.

Elodie spent most of her time picking at the fried chicken on her plate. He knew she must have been hungry, but she wasn't eating. He thought the t-shirt and leggings looked cute on her, but she tugged nervously at the old t-shirt as if worrying about being underdressed. He'd taken them out of his sister's closet because they looked comfortable. Of course, today would be one of the rare times the rest of his family sported business casual to dinner. Bruce had paint stains on his jeans and shirt. By that standard, he and Elodie were a perfect match.

"Perhaps your father's business has angered the wrong person," Margareta surmised. "Are ya sure the first incident happened when ya arrived here?"

"It's not her," Bruce said, not for the first time. "She didn't cause this."

His mother frowned at him. "We're only trying to reason what's happening. If we didn't cast the spell, then it had to come from somewhere."

"Maybe it's an accident," Raibeart piped in before swiping a bowl of mashed potatoes from the middle of the table. He piled them on his plate. "If it happens when ya draw, don't draw. Simple enough."

Katherine's brow furrowed, and she started to speak, only to catch herself.

"Asking Bruce not to draw is like asking the rest of us not to breathe." Cait sounded very much like a protective mother bear defending her cub. "I will not accept that he has to give up part of himself for a stupid spell."

"Ya keep calling it a spell, but it sounds like a

curse," Katherine said. The sound of her voice stopped everyone else from talking. She focused her sad brown eyes on Elodie. "None of ya can know what it's like to be trapped powerless, in a world that makes no sense, in a world ya can't control. I couldn't even begin to explain the feeling of waking up trapped in the cottage, decade after decade, with only the sound of my own voice to keep me company. It doesn't sound very different than being forced through one of those television boxes. So for ya to say Bruce shouldn't stop drawing because he likes the hobby is offensive to me. And I'm guessing it's offensive to Elodie as well. We didn't ask to fall in love with warlocks, and we didn't ask to be punished because of it. So you're going to stop treating her like she's done something wrong, and you're going to start acting like this family is the one who wronged her because, odds are, we're to blame. Not her."

"We—" Margareta began to protest.

"Not intentionally," Katherine amended, cutting Margareta off, "but as a consequence of who we are. Magick may be a gift, but it's more of a responsibility. I should not have to remind ya of that."

Elodie's fingers found his leg under the table.

He moved to hold her hand where the others couldn't see.

Katherine stood. "Elodie, it was a pleasure meeting ya. I hope only the best outcome for your troubles. Please excuse me."

"This has dredged up memories for her." Raibeart glanced at his mountain of potatoes as if contemplating bringing them with him before hurrying after his wife.

"Yeah, we should be going too," Iain said, pulling Jane to her feet. "We have an early morning delivery. Bruce, call me if ya need help, and I'll come back."

The table was quiet as Iain and Jane left. Margareta toyed with the food on her plate. Cait lifted the platter of fried chicken and offered everyone another piece. They refused.

"Of course, we're going to help ya, Elodie," Margareta said, her tone gentler than before. "And I did not mean to imply any of this was your fault."

"Aye," Cait agreed.

Bruce very much wanted to thank Katherine for her words.

"Thank—" Elodie's words were cut off by a screeching noise.

Bruce stood, prompting his father, Margareta, and Euann to do the same.

"What is that?" Cora asked, slower to stand. She went to the dining room window and looked out onto the darkened lawn. "Are those…?"

"Owls," Euann finished for her. "There has to be at least two dozen of them."

"Where did they come from?" Bruce went to the window to see for himself.

Euann was wrong. There were more than two dozen, and they kept coming. He saw the shadows of their movement in the branches of the giant oak on the front lawn. They perched along the top of the garage roof and on the hoods of cars. They came in a variety of shapes and sizes.

Elodie appeared next to him. She wrapped her fingers around his arm. "Is this an omen?"

"More birds," Cait said, sighing loudly.

"Muma Pădurii?" Margareta asked.

"Aye," Cait said. "Has to be. Who else would send this many owls to send a message?"

"What's the message?" Elodie asked.

"I don't know," Cait said. "I don't speak Romanian owl."

"It has to be a warning," Bruce reasoned. "No one sends a hundred owls as a friendly greeting."

"I thought there were protection spells," Elodie whispered to Bruce.

"There are," Euann defended. "It's why

they're all crowding into the front lawn and not flying into the house."

"How are we going to make it back to the motel?" she asked.

"Ya can't leave," Cait stated.

Elodie looked at Bruce. Her eyes searched his as if begging him to contradict his ma.

"We can try…" He looked at the birds. "But I think it's safer here."

Bruce knew he would find a way to take her to the motel if she insisted.

"Is there a way to contact Muma Pădurii to ask her what she wants?" Cora asked. "Can we call her?"

"If she even has a cellphone, it's probably because she ate some teenager carrying it," Euann answered.

"Euann!" Margareta swatted his arm. "No jokes while the owls are listening."

"Ah, look at poor Elodie's face. You're scaring her," his father sympathized. "Don't worry, dear one. There is no proof of her current dietary preferences. Times were very different in the Medieval period."

"Aye, now she probably invites wayward travelers to dinner on special occasions," Euann concluded.

"I…" Elodie shook her head and withdrew from the window.

"Euann!" Margareta scolded, louder than before.

"Do ya think the old crone will answer a cauldron?" Murdoch asked.

"I'll get the potion," Cait said, moving toward the library.

"I'll get the cauldron," Margareta added in exasperation, following her.

Bruce pulled Elodie with him to the foyer. He touched her cheek. "What are ya thinking?"

"I hope the crone doesn't eat me," she answered.

"She wouldn't dare try," Bruce swore. "The good news is that the elders will convince Muma Pădurii to stop whatever she's doing. With luck, that will be the end of the magickal chaos."

"I wish you'd just call it a curse because that's what it is." Elodie took a step back and looked toward the dining room.

Bruce glanced over to see Euann watching them.

"Sorry if our joking upset ya," Euann told Elodie.

"Thank you. I'm fine," Elodie answered politely.

"No. It's not fine," Bruce denied. "How would

ya feel if someone scared Cora with news of an ugly-arse cannibal coming to have her for a snack?"

Euann's expression dropped some, and he took a step back in retreat. "I apologize, Elodie."

"Thanks for that," Elodie said when they were again alone. "I know he wasn't being mean. Some people deflect fear with humor."

"Euann's not frightened." Bruce placed his hands on his hips. "He's just being an idiot."

"How can he not be...?" Elodie hugged her arms around her as if to make herself smaller. Then, answering herself, she said, "Because you're all used to this kind of thing. That's why none of you are panicking right now. You've been dealing with magickal problems for centuries."

"That's very astute of ya." Bruce nodded. "We have seen a lot of supernatural battles."

"And you understand how magick works. You know the rules." She rubbed her arms harder. "Don't lie to me. Don't try to make me feel better. Just tell me the truth. Is this situation bad?"

Bruce didn't want to answer her. He believed in honesty, but it warred with the need to protect her.

"Bruce," she insisted. "Please."

"Aye. The situation is bad," he answered. "But

only because we don't know who is threatening ya or why."

It wasn't what she wanted to hear. He saw that on her face. He wished he'd been able to lie to her.

"Thank you for telling me," Elodie swallowed nervously and glanced over her shoulder to the front door. "And you believe it might be Muma Pădurii who is doing this because you didn't take someone on a date?"

"I don't know." Bruce ran his hands through his hair. "I don't even know her cousin, Ullah. I didn't set it up. Maybe I should have gotten angrier with my ma when she started this match-making nonsense, but I didn't feel it mattered at the time. I figured I'd ride it out, and they'd lose interest."

Elodie nodded.

Bruce went to her, needing to touch her. "I didn't expect to find someone. I didn't expect ya. I could never have expected to find ya in a million years."

"There is a very logical part of my mind screaming right now that what you said is a line, that it can't be true." Elodie didn't back away from his approach.

"Good thing you're in a world of magick now." Bruce grinned, unable to help himself. He wanted to say sweet things to her. They were accurate, but he also liked seeing how her eyes dipped and her cheeks turned a slight shade of red. "Logic need not apply."

A small burst of laughter erupted, and she covered her mouth to stop it. "Oh, you're good. Very charming."

"Ya make it easy." He caressed her arms, rubbing them until she let go of herself, and they dropped to the side in a less protective stance. "I don't want ya to worry, Elodie. Hopefully, we can clear everything up with a cauldron call. They're setting up right now."

Bruce hoped it was the truth. Things were rarely that simple in the magickal world.

Elodie went to the window to look out. "The owls are still here."

"They're nocturnal. I suspect they'll hang out for a while."

"They're beautiful creatures," she said. "I've never seen anything like it. So many of them, so many different kinds. It's like they came from all over the world to congregate on your lawn."

Bruce had the passing thought of how he'd like to capture the moment. Not the birds, per se, but how she looked as she watched them. His hand twitched as if to summon a pencil, but he stopped it.

"I need to put the sketchpad in the vault. Just as a precaution," he said. "It'll be safe there."

Elodie continued watching the owls.

"Come with me?" he urged.

Elodie nodded and stepped away from the window. He took several steps toward the dining room when he heard the front door open. He swung around to find Elodie had gone outside.

"Elodie?" He rushed after her.

She walked toward the owls. Her arms hung limp at her sides.

"Elodie?" He reached her and grabbed her arm to stop her progress. Her eyes were glazed with white as she stared at the birds.

The owls took flight, circling overhead.

"Please accept humble apologies." Elodie's voice crackled.

"For what?" Bruce asked, confused. "Ya didn't do anything."

"Should you want a war, we cannot stop you," Elodie continued.

"Elodie, come on," Bruce tried to pull her with him, but her feet were locked on the ground. He tried lifting her. She didn't budge. He shot magick at the house, lighting up the protection barrier with blue to get the attention of those inside.

"Son?" Murdoch yelled.

"Help me!" Bruce hugged Elodie against him to protect her.

His father appeared next to them, gazing up at the bird-cluttered sky.

Murdoch wrapped his arms around the both of them. Bruce felt his father's magick creating a shield. "We got her."

Chapter Thirteen

Elodie had no idea how she'd gotten into the small one-room forest cottage, but that wasn't exactly a new feeling. Firelight shone over the earthen walls, showcasing the stringed rows of dried herbs and animal bones. Clay pots, some chipped, covered nearly every flat surface with space in the middle of the room for walking. Half-melted candles stood barren like dusty sculptures, their frozen drips hanging off stone ledges for an undetermined eternity.

"Please change the channel," she whispered.

Elodie tried to reason what this movie might be. Through the wavy panes of old glass, she saw black branches stretched over the sky like gnarled fingers. The night soaked up the sound until only the fireplace crackle broke through. Insects and animals remained quiet. She saw the outline of an owl sitting on a branch.

The smell from the fireplace cooking pot reminded her of rancid stew tinged with smoke from a partially clogged chimney. Opposite the fire was a thick mat on the floor for sleeping.

There was nowhere to hide. She could pry open the bolted door, but she had no idea what waited for her out in the night.

"Bruce?" she whispered.

The door unlatched itself and creaked open.

Was that him sending her a message?

Elodie instantly tried to leave. She didn't want to stay trapped in the eerie cottage.

Cold air blasted her as she exited. The fireplace had kept the cottage toasty. A 1980s rock band t-shirt and gray leggings were not the clothing of choice for wintery midnight excursions through a mystical forest. Elodie rubbed her bare arms.

Should she make a run for it?

Firelight came through the windows, flicking over the dark ground. Patches of snow accumulated through breaks in the thick trees. She wouldn't make it far if she became lost in the forest.

Elodie still didn't have shoes on, and the socks Bruce had given her did little to cushion her feet against the chilly forest floor. An owl hooted over-head, a lonely sound against the silence.

She noticed the firelight was brighter on one side of the cottage, a place where there were no windows, so she went slowly toward it. A firepit burned under a giant cauldron.

The slender outline of a woman hunched over it. Her back was to Elodie as her arms swayed back and forth with a giant stirring spoon. She lifted it from the liquid and dropped it on the ground.

Muma Pădurii?

Elodie did not want to look inside that cauldron. She tried to step back to hide quietly.

"Please accept humble apologies," Muma Pădurii said to the cauldron, her voice crackling and thick with a Romanian accent. "Should you want a war, we cannot stop you. However, that is not our wish. Ullah will be dealt with for her rudeness in rejecting the MacGregor suit, but she cannot be blamed."

Elodie stopped retreating to listen. Ullah rejected Bruce? She found herself creeping back to hear what was being said.

"I understand you must be disappointed. That is why I sent the owls to speak on our behalf," Muma Pădurii continued, and it sounded like Elodie was listening to one side of a phone call.

"But the heart wants what it wants, and Ullah's does not want the painted MacGregor who lives in a motel. We wish you luck in placing him."

Muma Pădurii grumbled indistinctly before spitting on the ground. Suddenly, the woman grabbed the edge of the cauldron and grunted as she pushed it over. Liquid sloshed onto the ground. The shadowed outline became more pronounced as the firelight brightened to show details of the fur and leather garments draping her figure.

Elodie stumbled back to hide. Suddenly arms gripped her like a vice, holding her tight from behind. She gasped and struggled to free herself. The landscape became a blur of motion.

"Elodie," Bruce said. "We got ya, love."

She stopped struggling and saw the forest was replaced by the MacGregor lawn. Bruce and his father held onto her. Owls took to flight, disappearing into the surrounding forest. Their grips loosened, and she stood free.

"What are we…?" She looked around, disorientated. "How did we get out here?"

"Owls used ya to help deliver their message. All the magick around ya must have opened ya up to be the easiest vessel," Murdoch said. "Let's go back inside."

"I saw her," Elodie said. "Muma Pădurii. I

was in her cottage. And she was talking to a cauldron about you, Bruce. She said Ullah didn't want to be with the painted MacGregor in a motel and was sorry about Ullah's rudeness in rejecting you."

Murdoch laughed. "I suppose that's better than Ullah taking a liking to ya, son. I don't know what your ma was thinking in proposing that alliance."

"So she doesn't think I rejected Ullah?" Bruce asked.

"I mean, I don't know. She didn't say she thought you did. Unless she was lying to save face or something. I could only hear her end of the conversation." Elodie let him lead her back toward the house. Her feet were still cold from Muma Pădurii's home.

"You're shivering," Bruce noted.

"Messengers take a lot out of people," Murdoch said. "Especially when you're not used to being a conduit."

When Elodie couldn't force her feet to move up the stairs, Bruce lifted her into his arms and held her against him as he carried her the rest of the way. The sound of their voices became muffled. Her body relaxed into him, and she was relieved to be back in Wisconsin in her new reality. Anything was better than a cannibal's cottage.

Chapter Fourteen

"Keep your voice down," Bruce ordered in a harsh whisper.

"Step out into the hall," someone answered.

"She's not leaving my sight," Bruce denied.

Elodie struggled to open her eyes. She saw Bruce's back as he stood in the doorway to the MacGregor guest room. Every part of her felt dull like her blood carried a heavy sedative. She lifted her head briefly, but it took too much effort. Her skin tingled as if she were crawling with magick, though she didn't see the telltale blue glow.

"It's not Muma Pădurii causing the problems." The second voice was Cait. "She answered the cauldron. She sent the birds as a peace offering because Ullah, if ya can believe it, thought she was too good for ya."

"I really don't care what a crone's twelfth cousin thinks of me, Ma," Bruce answered.

"Well, I'm insulted," Cait answered. "Ya were doing her a favor by taking her out on a pity date."

"If that is how ya choose to think of it, I can't stop ya," Bruce said. "I couldn't care less about Ullah if she's not causing the attack on Elodie. Are ya sure it's not Muma Pădurii?"

"Aye. I'm positive. She's old-fashioned when it comes to betrothals. She's more worried about us being offended." Cait's voice sounded muffled. "She doesn't want ya to feel jilted."

Elodie tried to speak but only managed a small moan.

"Then we don't know why this is happening." Bruce let loose a frustrated sigh and slapped his palm against the doorframe before catching himself. "Can ya please ensure the sketchpad is in the safest vault? I don't want anyone mistakenly drawing on it. Until we know the parameters of this curse, we can't be too safe."

Cait's response was lost.

"All I know is that Elodie did not bring this on herself. So go through that entire list of women ya tried to set me up with and start finding who's responsible." Bruce shut the door.

Elodie listened to the latch click before succumbing to the magickal sedation.

When she again opened her eyes, some of her energy had returned, and she was able to maneuver herself into sitting against the headboard. Bruce was instantly by her side, helping her get comfortable.

"How do ya feel?" He stroked the hair back from her face.

"Happy to not be cooking in a stew right now," she mumbled, trying to be funny even though the joke fell flat.

Elodie wore the same borrowed pants and shirt, but the socks were gone. She felt the weight of the covers pressing down on her bare feet. She watched her toes move like tiny animals beneath the silk.

"My feet feel numb," she said.

Bruce instantly went to the foot of the bed and dug her feet out from beneath the covers. He sat and pulled a foot into his lap and began rubbing his thumb against the arch.

Elodie watched him in surprise. Her lids fell heavy over her eyes as numbness turned to pleasurable tingling when he moved to lift her other foot. "You're good at this. If billionaire warlock motel owner doesn't work out, you might have a shot as a masseuse."

"We owned nail salons in New York. I helped manage them for a time. They taught me all their tricks." Bruce winked. "I am a man of many talents."

"Really?" she arched a brow.

"Aye, I'll show ya." He held out his hand and materialized a bottle of purple nail polish. He moved as if to paint her toes, only to stop before the tip of the polish brush touched her. He twisted the bottle's lid back on and made it disappear. "Sorry, love. I was going to paint little cityscapes on your toes, but I shouldn't do anything creative."

"Ah, that sucks. This current reality doesn't allow me to get fancy toes."

Bruce arched a brow. "This is reality-reality."

"How do I know this moment is real?" Elodie gazed at him, smiling softly. "It feels like a dream."

"A good dream, I hope." He resumed rubbing her feet. Tiny blue sparks of his magick came from his fingers, stimulating her nerves and causing a chain reaction up her leg. His green eyes met hers. They seemed to glow with an inner light, and she realized it was the blue of his magick swirling inside of him.

"What happens now?" Elodie watched his hands as they glided beyond her foot to her calf.

He rubbed her through the tighter material of the leggings. Her breathing deepened.

"I must have lost my touch if ya can't guess my intentions," Bruce teased, moving to her other calf to give it the same tingling treatment.

She lightly kicked at him, laughing. "I didn't mean this."

"I like seeing ya smile." Bruce continued to work his massage magick, slipping higher up her leg to stroke her lower thigh.

"I heard you with your mom." Elodie tried to keep her mind focused, but it was difficult when he touched her like that. "We're back to square one. We don't know who cursed me or why."

"I promise we'll find the answer. Every MacGregor is being brought up to speed. Every one of us is looking to protect ya." Bruce appeared so earnest that she felt compelled to believe him.

But what if he couldn't figure it out?

What if the magick pulled her away again?

Elodie never felt it coming. She just blinked, and she was someplace new. Every time she closed her eyes, she feared what would await her when she opened them.

Bruce moved back and forth between her legs, massaging her lower thighs, then the upper. She waited for him to pull the leggings out of the way, but he didn't. He just worked his way to her hips before reaching beneath her to rub her lower back. His legs straddled hers, careful not to put too much weight on her.

"Turn over," he urged.

Elodie didn't hesitate. She rolled onto her stomach and pushed her pillow aside to lay flat. Bruce massaged under the t-shirt, stroking her back. His tingling fingers worked a knot in her shoulder.

Elodie kept her eyes open, not wanting to slip from this moment. Each second felt lucky.

"Do ya still feel numb?" he asked, his voice low and husky.

"I feel tingly." A tiny laugh escaped her. "And relaxed."

His hands rubbed deeper. "I was hoping for tingly and aroused."

"That too." She wiggled beneath him.

He let her turn over to face him before settling back down to trap her legs.

Elodie ran her fingers into his overgrown hair. She liked that he had a Bohemian feel to his appearance, not like the other MacGregors.

Unlike most of the wealthy people she met, Bruce wasn't trying to impress anyone. When he spoke, his words weren't filled with pretension and arrogance. Like her, he came from money, but he didn't flaunt it. Instead, he lived away from the mansion in a motel. And it wasn't even a fancy hotel. It was a blue-collar family road trip pit stop. Maybe that's what they had in common. They were both straddling two worlds and had both sought a life with fewer complications.

"I love that I can't tell what you're thinking," Bruce said.

"I'm thinking about you." She ran her thumb over his bottom lip.

He leaned down to kiss her. Her thumb came with him, pressing between their lips. She caressed his cheek before running her hands into his hair to hold him against her. They deepened the kiss.

Elodie stirred beneath him. His hand found her naked waist as he shifted his weight. She gripped his shirt.

"Do the clothing thing," she whispered.

He grinned. She felt the slither of clothing melt off her body. It pooled like liquid next to them. When it finished, they were naked, and their clothes were piled messily on the bed.

"That has to be the coolest thing magick can do," Elodie said as his mouth moved down her neck.

"For all the chaos, there are a few perks," Bruce agreed between kisses. He nibbled at her earlobe. The light caress tickled, and she squirmed her ear away.

"What other magick tricks do you have?" Elodie challenged.

Bruce lifted his hand to show magick swirling his fingers before reaching between them. He drew his hand down her stomach to the apex of her thighs. Gently parting the folds of her sex, he let the tingling sensation wash over her in waves.

Elodie gasped in pleasure. Her hand glided along his naked hip to instinctively pull him closer. The feel of his arousal brushed her leg as he shifted to put his legs between her thighs. Her fingers curled around the bottom crease of his ass as she tried to bring him closer.

Bruce resisted. Instead, he lightly stroked her with his fingers, letting his magick do most of the work. It encircled her clit and caused her to shake with anticipation.

This was more than physical pleasure. With each stroke, she felt his magick connecting them. It wasn't logical, but it was pure instinct. They did not have the history of years, but that didn't seem to matter. She knew she could trust him. She knew she belonged in this bed with him. She knew *him* on an emotional level.

Bruce licked at her mouth, playfully begging for another kiss. When their lips met, it was fireworks—sizzling hot sparks of magick that exploded around them, unable to be contained.

Their movements became frenzied. She reached between them to cup his arousal. Her legs rubbed along his thighs.

The blue fireworks rained down on them, each tiny spark like a small pinch. A pulse of energy came from his hand as a finger dipped inside her body, jolting violently up her sex to seize her stomach muscles. She cried out in surprise as the orgasm ripped through her. She'd never felt anything like the rush of it.

Elodie's heart pounded, and she tried to catch her breath. "Oh, oh, wow."

"How was that for a magick trick?" Bruce kissed her neck.

Elodie chuckled and could only manage another, "Wow."

"Happy to hear it, love." He kept kissing her neck.

Elodie felt his full arousal brushing her thigh. He had yet to find his release, but he didn't pressure her for more. This was the most amazing man she had ever met, so giving of himself.

Bruce's hands and mouth began exploring her body. In the glow of the aftermath, she weakly caressed him where she could reach. Her heartbeat began to slow even as her desire built.

Hands cupped her breasts. His lips grazed over her nipples before venturing along her stomach, licking a trail down to her center heat. She focused on each second, anticipating where his mouth might go next, and was surprised when it happened.

Bruce kissed the sensitive flesh he found buried between her thighs. Only when she was writhing beneath him in perfect agony, begging him for more, did he make his way back up her body.

He entered her, deep and hard. She cried out in pleasure. Their bodies glistened with magick. She felt his power swimming inside of her.

Their hips rocked. With each thrust, the magick jumped off their skin like glitter, sprinkling on the bed. The fire surged in the fireplace as if announcing his release. Climax came over her in trembling waves. She held him tight against her, wrapping her legs and arms around him to keep him inside.

She collapsed on the bed. Bruce rolled next to her, sitting up on his arm.

"How are you upright now?" she whispered, trying to reach for his face, but her hand dropped weakly before making contact.

"I feel like I can take over the world." He grinned, nuzzling her neck playfully.

"But how?" she suppressed a yawn.

"Unlike the slow pull of nature, sexual energy hits my magick like a lightning bolt. Hard, intense, but it doesn't last as long." He finally laid down next to her.

"Like a sugar rush?" She closed her eyes and quickly opened them again because she didn't want to disappear from his side.

"Exactly like that," he agreed.

"I don't think I can stay awake," Elodie mumbled. "I'm so tired."

"Sleep. I promise I'll stay right here. I'm not leaving your side." He kissed her temple.

Her eyes closed, and she couldn't force them back open. "Don't do the protection spell again. I didn't like feeling like a ghost. No one could see me."

He pulled her into his arms, holding her tight. "Maybe this time I'll make a protective bubble around both of us. Then no one can find us. We'll be in our own little safe world as we go around haunting people, eavesdropping on secret conversations. No one will be able to get to us."

"Ok," she whispered. "We can do that one."

Chapter Fifteen

Bruce watched Elodie sleep, unable to rest himself. He didn't want her to know the deep fear inside him. If Muma Pădurii and Ullah didn't bring on this curse, he had no clue where to look next. Aye, his family was helping search, but that didn't calm his fear.

The stupid blind dates were the only new happening in his life that could have affected him. Otherwise, he'd been keeping to himself, reading and painting. Well, and annoying his sister, but that was hardly new.

He was ready to fight anyone who tried to hurt Elodie, but first, he had to figure out who he was fighting against. He'd gladly give his life for hers. In a few short days, Elodie had become his everything. He could not live without her.

Life had been quiet. He couldn't think of a single creature he'd turned into an enemy, let alone a supernatural with enough power to summon a curse that could alter reality.

Correction. Life had been quiet *recently*.

The problem with supernaturals that have immortal lifespans was that they had a long time to hold a grudge. Bruce would have to examine his entire life. That was no easy prospect. The beauty of time was that it faded some memories. A person couldn't carry hundreds of years with them, clinging to each fleeting moment. Only the significant events stuck out. That didn't mean he didn't try.

Bruce stared at Elodie, watching her breathe, scared that she'd disappear if he took his eyes off her. It didn't matter that the house was protected or that his family was nearby to help. The threat was real, and it was against everything that mattered.

Her cheeks appeared flushed, so he lifted his hand to tamp down the heat from the fireplace. He watched the shift of light on her features as they shadowed. Habit caused him to materialize a pencil. It twirled in his fingers before he sent it back to where it had come. Giving up his passion for art would be difficult, but it would be nothing compared to keeping her safe.

He thought about wrapping his magick around them in a bubble. He'd been joking, sort of, but the idea had appeal.

"Forever," he whispered, stroking a lock of her hair from her face. "That is where I want to live with ya. Inside of forever."

He had to figure out why this was happening. He had to think.

When he was a boy, maybe eleven or twelve, several people from East Lothian, Scotland, had been accused of playing with the devil's magick in St Andrew's Auld Kirk in North Berwick. It had been dangerous times, and the elders had hidden them from the hunters. The hunters were long dead, but they had descendants.

No. Why would they wait five hundred years to do this? It didn't make sense. The same could be said for all the witch trials over the centuries.

About twenty years after that, he and Erik had messed with a vampire den. They drank too much and thought trapping them in their cave magickally was hilarious. Unfortunately, the vampire king was supposed to be married, and it became an ordeal. Most of that gang would still be alive. Well, undead but alive.

No. This hardly seemed like vampires. Their approaches tended to include more blood.

Werewolf bikers? Bruce had bailed his cousin

Niall out of trouble a few times. Aside from being a warlock, Niall had been born a werewolf, and there was a time he'd fallen into a questionable crowd.

No. Not that. It needed to be someone who could harness that kind of power.

Goblins? Leprechauns? Sirens? Fairies?

No. Sure, he'd pissed a few of them off in his time, but it had to be someone disciplined who could access the type of magick needed to create a curse.

Wizards? Demons? Necromancers? Alchemists? The ancient Druid clan?

But why? They all had the power, but he couldn't think of how he'd wronged them.

Round and round his mind went as Bruce tried to come up with an answer. He couldn't. If it wasn't him, then it was someone from his family. It had to be their fault. Elodie was human and did not come from magick. This couldn't be random. It felt too targeted.

Guilt filled him. He gazed at her sleeping face, wondering how long he could stay awake watching over her. He spread out beside her and rolled onto his side, observing her chest lift and fall. The rhythm of it comforted him. Up and down, up and down, soft and even.

"Forever," he whispered, praying it was one promise he could keep.

Chapter Sixteen

Elodie kicked the covers off her legs and jerked upright to sit on the bed. Sweat poured off her body, and she felt as if she'd just broken a fever. She looked around, confused and scared as to what was happening now.

She recognized the motel room first, then her duffel bag. The pile of dirty clothes was where she'd left them near the bathroom floor. The bed was messy from being slept in.

"Bruce?" she called, rushing to the bathroom to look for him. He wouldn't have left her, at least not willingly. "Bruce?"

She saw movement and jumped, startled, until she realized it was her own naked reflection staring back at her. Her cheek was slightly discolored where the zombie bait farmer had punched her, and various bruises littered her flesh.

Elodie took comfort in seeing the injuries. They had to mean she didn't fever-dream Bruce or what happened between them.

Why was she here? Now? Did this mean the curse was over, and her life just reset?

She crossed to the curtains to peek out. The car Bruce had doodled on was gone. Bright daylight covered the motel parking lot. The Hotel Motel sign showed that they had vacancies, and the parking lot looked emptier than before.

The sound of skipping echoed down the sidewalk as a child ran ahead of his father. The man's eyes found her watching and widened before he quickly swept in front of his kid to redirect him in the other direction.

Elodie glanced down and realized she'd unintentionally flashed him. Thankfully the kid hadn't seen. She jerked the curtains closed and hurried for her bag.

"Please be over. Please be over," she repeated as she tugged on blue jeans and a green long-sleeve t-shirt. If she did take another mystical trip, she wanted to be dressed for it.

Ding.

Elodie glanced toward the bed at the sound of her phone as she pulled on socks and sneakers.

A few seconds passed before another *ding*.

"Bruce?" she went to the bed and threw the blankets aside as she looked for the device.

Ding.

"Hold on, I'm coming," she muttered.

Finally, she grabbed the comforter and shook it. The phone fell out. She slid onto the floor and sat against the bed, bracing her feet against the wall beneath the window.

The battery was low. She touched the notification window to bring up her text messages. They were all from Roberto. She scrolled to the top of the long message list and began reading.

"Call."

"Maledico tibi."

"Ignore that."

"Fundraiser tonight."

"Fundraiser in an hour."

"Not cool, princess."

"Answer your phone. Your mother wants to speak to you."

"Pick up."

"Why aren't you picking up?"

"Magazine shoot Tuesday. Confirm."

"Tuesday confirmed. Be here."

"You better be in a ditch somewhere without service. Unacceptable."

"Magazine moved to Thurs at two."

They kept going, and she stopped reading to scroll to the end.

"Hard truth time."

"You're selfish. Your mother needed you."

"Don't bother coming Thursday."

"Aranearum."

"Stupid autocorrect."

"Are you getting this?"

Elodie frowned. Two days' worth of messages and not one text asked how she was or if she needed anything. They knew she'd been in the emergency room after being bitten by a snake. They knew she was having a rough time. And if she wasn't responding to messages, they should have assumed something might be wrong. What stung more was that none of the messages were from her parents. They were all Roberto.

She checked her missed calls. Only one, and it was from Roberto's number.

Elodie frowned and tossed the phone behind her head onto the bed.

For a moment, the loneliness came rushing back like a wave, flooding her soul. The despondency had haunted her throughout her entire life. It felt worse now that she had met Bruce and knew what something better could feel like.

"Bruce." She pushed up from the floor. This

was his motel. Green Vallis wasn't a large town. She could find him.

Elodie started for the bathroom, only to stop and grab her phone. Voice texting, she answered Roberto, "*Still in Green Vallis, WI. Not available for appointments. I told you that already if you'd bother to listen, princess. Hard truth time. You're a kiss ass, and your real name is Jim. You're not fooling anyone. My mother is selfish, and my father is self-absorbed. If they want to speak to me, they can call me themselves. Otherwise, fuck all the way off.*"

Elodie stared at the message. Her finger hovered over the send button. There was so much more she wanted to say and many things she shouldn't. Sighing, she deleted part of the message and sent, "*Still in Green Vallis, WI. Not available for appointments.*"

She tossed her phone back on the bed. There was no point in fighting with her mom's assistant. She doubted her mother would take her side over Roberto-Jim's if it came down to it. And she didn't need more drama to deal with. Right now, she needed to reconnect with Bruce.

A sense of urgency came over her at the idea that this reality might not last. Elodie hurried to the bathroom and brushed her hair into a small bun. She splashed cold water on her face. She rubbed sleep from her eyes and blotted with a towel. Something tickled the back of her hand. She dropped the towel and instantly swatted the sensation. A spider fell off her into the porcelain sink.

"Ugh." She gave a slight shiver of disgust and stepped away from the small attacker.

She instinctively reached for the faucet to flush it down the sink. Before she could turn the water back on, another spider crawled out of the spout.

She lifted her hands in retreat. "Never mind. Sink's yours, boys."

A small *tink-tink* sounded in the bathtub. She turned to find two more dark spots crawling up the side of the tub. They were soon joined by friends dropping from the tub faucet onto the cap of the metal drain.

Tink-tink-tink-tink.

"I really hate this curse." Elodie stumbled backward, away from them. A few spiders turned into an army. They crawled from the tub and sink, swarming onto the floor.

Elodie backed through the motel room. Spiders emerged from empty plug-ins and from behind the mirror. They crawled from behind the television and dangled like webbed chandelier crystals from the light fixture. The covers moved, carried on the backs of what she could only assume were more of the little demons.

One dropped on her shoulder, and she flung it off. Seconds later, more landed on her head. She swatted at her hair as she ran for the door, not that she could see it under the swarming mass covering it.

Elodie hit the knob several times before jerking it open and running outside. Sounds of disgust and fear escaped her in partial whines, partial moans, and partial screams. She danced along the sidewalk, hitting her hands against her body to stop them from crawling on her. She shivered and jerked. Everything blurred, and she was too wigged out to stop and access her surroundings.

"Elodie?" Maura blocked the sidewalk, holding an armful of clean towels.

Elodie stopped, freezing mid-erratic dance move. Her hands were in her hair, and she gave a strained smile. "Hi. Maura. Hi."

"Are ya…? Is Bruce here?" Maura asked.

"I don't know." Elodie still felt as if they crawled beneath her t-shirt. She slapped her arms. "No. There's an arachnid army trying to put me in," she paused to swipe at her neck, "a web cocoon. Sink. Bathtub."

"Arachnid army?" Maura looked behind her at the sidewalk. "I don't see anything."

Elodie turned to find the sidewalk clear. "Spiders. In my room. Everywhere."

"Is this another night terror?" Maura frowned and moved toward Elodie's open motel room door.

"Don't…" Elodie reached out and tried to stop her from going in. Her heart pounded violently from the fearful attack.

Maura stepped inside a few feet. "I don't see anything."

"They were…" Elodie looked in. They were gone. "I'm not crazy. They were real. They were right here."

"I didn't say ya were crazy," Maura answered. She set the clean towels down on the dresser beside the television. "Is this part of the curse Bruce was asking us about?"

Elodie nodded. She was slower to reenter the room. Somehow having Maura in there made her feel a little better. Still, she lingered close to the door.

"Did they bite ya?" Maura looked her over.

"I…" Elodie pulled up the shirt's long sleeves to check her arms before reaching to feel her neck. Her gaze darted around, searching for movement. She shook her head in denial. Even now, she felt them crawling on her and couldn't stop herself from rubbing her arms and stomach to make the sensation stop. Her eyes watered. "I hate this. I just want it to go away."

"Oh, hey now, don't cry," Maura soothed. She had a comforting presence. "We'll get this figured out. I thought ya were staying at the house where ya were protected. Where's my brother?"

"I went to sleep at the house, but then I woke up here." Elodie gestured around the room. "I don't know where I'll be from one moment to the next or what horror will be awaiting me when I get there."

"Do ya have any idea who might be doing this to ya?" Maura asked.

Elodie shook her head. "Bruce thought it was a relative of one of his blind dates, but that turned out to be a dead end. They're still trying to figure out who has a grudge against your family."

Maura's lips pressed together as she tried not to smirk. "Yeah. That's going to be a long list."

Elodie felt her shoulders slump as she hugged her stomach.

"And on your list?" Maura asked.

"What list?"

Maura tilted her head. "Who has a grudge against ya?"

"No one," Elodie answered, shrugging. "I mean, I don't do anything important."

Maura studied her, her brow furrowed. "What do ya do? For work?"

"Wannabe writer," Elodie answered, almost

embarrassed to admit she lived off family money. She glanced at the phone on the bed. "I attend social obligations for my parents."

"What does that mean?"

"I've been over this with Bruce. He thinks it has something to do with…" Elodie gestured helplessly toward Maura. "MacGregors."

"Aye, probably," Maura agreed. "Tell me anyway. What did ya mean by social obligations for your parents?"

Elodie hated not having an answer. She hated it even more that she had nothing to do with the problem in the first place. If it wasn't her doing, she didn't have the tools to fix it.

"It's like a full-time job, posing as the happy daughter and charming corporate so-and-sos at parties and fundraisers," she explained. "I mean, I guess some of them might not like my family. My mom is pretty much a socialite who likes her picture taken. My dad owns an investment firm with corporate clients. I have no reason to suspect anything shady happening there. More importantly, I have no reason to suspect anyone knows anything about magick."

Elodie went to pick up her phone off the bed like it was somehow evidence to prove her boring life. She tapped the screen, but the battery had died.

"Half the conversations I have with my parents are via text messages through my mom's assistant," she continued. "He's a little peeved at me right now because I didn't agree to do some magazine shoot. He gets mad and starts typing gibberish. I mean, it's stupid. The last time I went, they didn't even use any of the photos I was in. It was a complete waste of time."

"May I?" Maura held out her hand.

"Why?" It felt a little evasive to have someone else reading her messages.

"Because bad magick is affecting a guest at my motel. And I have never seen Bruce worry about a woman the way he was worrying over ya when he called me. If there is even the smallest chance I can figure it out, I'll take it."

Elodie handed her the phone. She didn't have anything to hide. "It's dead. My charger is in my—"

"I got it." Maura pointed the phone toward a plug-in. The screen lit up.

Elodie watched as the battery went to full power within seconds. "Neat trick."

"Where're the messages?"

Elodie reached over and pulled up Roberto's messages.

"Are ya getting this? Stupid autocorrect,"

Maura read the text messages from the bottom up. "Ara—"

"He typos all the time," Elodie interjected. "Just skip it."

"Aranearum," Maura read with a frown. She stopped reading each one and started scrolling faster. She stopped and said, "Maledico tibi."

"What?"

"Who is this Roberto guy?" Maura asked as she looked at more messages.

"My mom's assistant." Elodie frowned.

"Hard truth. You're selfish. Don't come. Ya better be in a ditch somewhere without service. Unacceptable?" Maura shook her head. "This guy doesn't care for ya. I have never had a family employee that spoke to me like this. Who is he?"

"As I said, he's my mom's personal assistant." Elodie felt a tickle and swatted at her arm. When Maura's expression made it clear that she wanted more information, Elodie added, "His real name is Jim something. I think he said he's from Duluth or someplace like that originally. He's been working for my mom for a couple of years. He is pretty much tangled up into every aspect of her life."

"Duluth? You're sure?"

"Yeah. Minnesota." Elodie looked at her phone screen, wondering what she wasn't seeing.

"And he hates ya?"

"I wouldn't say hate," Elodie defended.

"No, this man," Maura held up the phone for emphasis, "resents ya. I promise ya that."

"No, he just talks like that...," Elodie rubbed her arms. She really wanted out of the spider room. "He doesn't mean dead in a ditch, literally. It's just his way of saying he's upset that I'm not agreeing with his stupid appointments."

"*Aranearum* is Latin for spiders. *Maledico tibi* literally means I curse ya." Maura kept looking. "*Evanesce* means disappear. *Arena* can mean sand."

"But that's just autocorrect mistakes," Elodie said weakly.

Maura tapped the phone a few times and then held it to her ear. "Bruce, calm down. Stop yelling. She's here at the motel. We're on our way to the house. Don't leave."

"Bruce..." Elodie reached toward Maura, wanting to talk to Bruce.

Maura didn't give her the phone back. The device lit with yellow magick, and Elodie saw the battery drain. Maura put it in her pocket.

"Come on," Maura instructed, leaving the room.

"So is that it? We just turn off the phone?" Elodie followed, confused.

"He texted ya spiders, and spiders came,"

Maura said. "If we stop his texts from arriving, we might buy some time."

Roberto-Jim? Seriously?

Elodie followed Maura, mainly because the woman seemed confident in what she was doing. Plus, she was taking her back to Bruce.

Maura materialized keys as she opened the door to a small compact car. She tossed them at the ignition, and they floated into place. The engine started as she slid into the driver's seat.

Elodie glanced nervously around the parking lot before getting in the car.

"So," Maura said as she sped out of the parking lot. "Ya and my brother."

The tires squealed as she took a corner.

"Yeah," Elodie managed, bracing herself on the door.

"I'm happy to hear that," Maura said. "He's been alone a long time. Not sure what ya see in him, but there is no accounting for taste."

Elodie held on tighter as Maura hit the gas, and they zoomed across a yellow light. "He's…"

She couldn't think of the right thing to say to Bruce's sister.

He's sexy. He's amazing. He's everything.

"I'm teasing," Maura said.

They turned up the drive that would take them to the mansion. Maura accelerated. The tires kicked up dirt behind them like a cloud. Only when they were near the top did Maura slow down.

Bruce stood on the lawn waiting for them. The moment they appeared, he instantly ran toward the car. Elodie had her hand on the handle before the car came to a complete stop. She opened the door and hopped out.

"Why did ya leave the house? I would have taken ya to the motel," Bruce insisted, pulling her against him. He wore a black long-sleeve shirt and a kilt with boots. "I was worried sick trying to find ya."

"I didn't mean to. I woke up in the motel," Elodie explained. She wrapped her arms around him. "I thought the house was protected."

"It is." Bruce looked at his sister. "Thanks for bringing her."

"Well, like always, it's up to me to come to your rescue," Maura quipped. She pulled Elodie's phone from her pocket and held it in the air. "I come bearing answers to your problem."

Bruce kept his arm around Elodie as they followed Maura into the house. "Are ya sure you're ok? Did anything bad happen?"

"Spiders," she shivered. "Lots and lots of spiders."

Chapter Seventeen

Bruce refused to leave Elodie's side. He felt guilty for falling asleep. It hadn't felt as if his eyes had been closed long, but the second he opened them, she was gone, and daylight came through the window. He'd searched everywhere for her, even looking inside the paintings hanging around the mansion for clues.

They sat at the dining room table with his parents, Margareta, Raibeart, Euann, and Iain. Margareta poured coffee from an antique silver serving set like they were having a lovely brunch. Cait followed behind her handing out slices of coffee cake and cloth napkins. Raibeart didn't wait for everyone to be served before he picked up his cake and took a large bite. Euann at least picked up his fork and waited. Bruce pushed his plate aside as a symbolic gesture, not caring for food at the moment. This was too important, and they were wasting time with niceties.

"To answer your question from the front lawn, Elodie." Maura held everyone's attention as she leaned over to let Margareta pour her coffee. "The curse was placed on ya before ya entered the house. That is why the protection spells didn't work to keep ya inside. Ya were already infected."

"Maura, ya said ya know what's happening," Bruce insisted. "Stop with dramatic effect. Which one of us brought this on her?"

"The ego of men," Maura muttered. "Why does it have to be about ya, Bruce?"

"It's magick. Of course, it's about this family." Bruce gripped Elodie's hand in his on top of the table. "Elodie is an innocent. She's sweet. She's perfect. She'd never do anything against anyone."

Elodie gave him a small smile at the compliment before turning back to Maura.

"Ya are so sure it had to be something against our family that caused this," Maura countered. "I swear, male warlock ego is the worst."

"Maura," their mother warned. "Enough with the dramatics. Do ya know what caused this?"

Maura took Elodie's phone and placed it on the table. "I present to ya a high-tech curse."

Euann dropped his fork and stood. He rushed

around the table to pick up the phone. "Ya don't say? How?"

Euann had a thing for tech gadgets and didn't try to hide his excitement.

"Elodie has been getting texts from someone who works for her ma," Maura explained. *"Aranearum. Maledico tibi. Evanesce.* Things like that. All short. All in Latin. All disguised as spelling errors buried in distracting nonsense."

"Spiders?" Bruce looked at Elodie in question. "Ya were saying something about spiders before."

Elodie nodded and started rubbing her arm. She gave a visible shiver. "This morning in the motel room. Thousands of them."

"High-tech Latin curse," Euann said, examining the dead phone in fascination. "How very ghost in the machine."

"Whatever that means," Iain muttered, drinking his coffee.

"Ya going to eat that?" Raibeart swiped the coffee cake off Iain's plate and shoved it in his mouth.

"Hey!" Iain set his coffee cup down.

"Too slow," Raibeart taunted with a mouth full of food.

"I've heard of cursed objects, but a cursed digital message?" Cait put another slice of cake in front of Iain to replace the one that was stolen. "Euann, is that even a real thing?"

"Oh, aye," Euann said. "I'm telling ya, technology's uses for magick are fascinating. People can program all sorts of things nowadays. With a few clicks, they can put on digital glamours to look like anyone they want. One search and ya can learn about any obscure topic ya want—"

"Like why Iain's so ugly." Raibeart interrupted, stealing Iain's cake a second time and shoving it in his mouth.

"Sure," Euann agreed. "There's all kinds of information on—"

Iain took Euann's cake off his plate and launched it across the table at his brother. Euann ducked.

"Eh." Margareta pointed at her sons in warning. Iain picked up his coffee and hid behind a drink. Euann grinned and shrugged.

Bruce ignored them as he stared at Elodie's hand in his.

"As I was saying before I was interrupted, programmers can program all sorts of things nowadays," Euann said. "It stands to reason some supernatural figured out a way to use tech as a delivery method for spells. Ya know, the other day, I found a how-to, step-by-step article on how to enact an actual weather magick spell. Not strong, but still. Someone could call a raincloud or two with it."

Euann started to point the phone toward the wall as if to charge it. Maura snatched it from him before he could.

"Rainclouds aside," Maura dismissed Euann's turn of conversation, "this personal assistant uses texts to amplify his curse. I'm guessing he keeps his tools somewhere safe, like a magickal home base. I turned off the phone to keep him from sending his curse through. I doubt this stops it altogether, but that might take away some of his control."

"Who is this person?" Bruce asked Elodie.

Margareta and Cait gave up on serving and took their seats.

All eyes turned to her, and she averted her gaze toward him. "Roberto. Well, *Jim.* My mom hired him to help keep her schedule and run errands. He's just a guy. He wears skinny jeans with gemstones and over-gels his hair."

She glanced nervously at his family before looking back at him.

"I didn't do anything to him," Elodie insisted. "I swear. I don't know why he'd do this. I don't know *how* he's doing this."

"We believe ya," Bruce assured her.

"Aye, lassie, anyone can see you're sweet as a

honeycomb," Raibeart came to her defense. "Now, don't ya worry. We're going to dangle this Jim over hot lava until he removes the curse. Just tell us where he is, and we'll bring him to the nearest volcano."

Elodie leaned closer to Bruce's chair and drew their hands off the table to rest on her knee. "I just want this to be over."

"Then we'll go have a conversation with Jim," Bruce said. "Where is he?"

"My mother is at the Manhattan penthouse right now," Elodie said. "He'll be with her."

Bruce turned to his mother. "I'm going to need the jet."

"Of course," his ma said. "I'll arrange it now."

"Wait," Margareta lifted her hand to stop Cait from standing. "It might be unsafe to send someone under a curse into the sky. Who knows what would happen thirty thousand feet into the air?"

"Oh, aye, gremlins." Raibeart motioned at the serving tray with coffee cake on it. He wiggled his fingers, and it slid closer to him.

"Gremians," Margareta corrected.

"No, gremlins," Raibeart said. "Horrible mechanics."

"Gremlins?" Elodie repeated, worried.

Bruce silently willed Raibeart to stop helping as he shook his head. "No."

"I agree with your aunt. I don't want to fly cursed." Elodie dropped his hand and reached for the coffee.

"We'll drive. It's only fifteen hours." Bruce stood. "We'll leave now."

"I'll need someone to watch Tina," Maura said as she pushed to her feet to join him.

"Go with your brother. I'll watch my little angel grandbaby," Cait said. "I'll tell Rory to meet ya there. He insisted on flying back with Jennifer when I told him ya needed him."

"Rory is Bruce's twin brother," Margareta explained to Elodie.

"Take my car," Euann tossed keys to the Pontiac at Bruce. "It's faster than yours. It'll cut down your drive time."

"I'll get ya the code to the Manhattan house," Iain said. "The fridge will be empty, but the potion cabinet is stocked. Restraints are in the vault if ya need them."

Elodie held onto her coffee cup. Her breathing was a little too steady as if she counted the seconds in and out. "If Jim did this, does that mean he's not a human?"

"We're not sure," Maura said.

"But we're going to find out," Bruce assured her.

"Is my mother safe?" Elodie asked.

Bruce didn't want to lie to her, but the truth would only scare her.

"The texts I read didn't appear to threaten your ma," Maura said.

"I'll pack road snacks." Margareta went to the kitchen.

Elodie kept breathing. One two in. One two out. One two in…

"Hey, we have a plan," Bruce whispered. He put his forehead against her temple. "We know who the enemy is. This will end."

She nodded. "But, if something happens to me…"

"It won't," he swore. If something happened to her, then nothing would matter. The world would stop.

"If something happens…" she insisted. "If this curse takes me before we stop it, promise me you'll get Jim away from my family. My mother and I might not always get along, but she doesn't deserve… Just promise me you'll help her."

Bruce nodded. "We'll stop him."

Chapter Eighteen

Elodie tried not to watch the blur of the landscape outside the car's window as they crossed the border from Wisconsin into Illinois. The high speed and stress of the situation caused her stomach to churn. Whatever magick Euann had put on his car made the drive go faster. They managed to hit perfectly flowing traffic the entire way, even as they headed into the Chicago area. And, miraculously, they never had to stop to refuel.

Jim.

The man's name rolled around in her head, mocking her.

Fucking fake Roberto. Fucking Jim.

Seriously?

The big scary evil threat was… Jim?

Maura slept in the back of the car as Bruce drove. She had brought a blanket and pillow with her on the trip.

Elodie had the front passenger seat. She stared at the center lines marking the pavement as they rolled past. Between them, in a cupholder, was her dead phone. It sat like a horrible reminder of what this road trip was all about.

"You're quiet," Bruce observed.

She loved looking at his face. A little less than that, she loved looking at his kilt. She'd been fond of the paint-smudged jeans, but there was a romantic hero quality to a kilt that could not be denied. It had been one of the few things on this trip that distracted her mind.

"I don't want to wake up Maura." It was true, but only a tiny part of the truth.

They sped past the Chicago skyline. The wide lanes of thick traffic naturally parted, so what would have normally taken hours of gridlock became as easy as a Sunday drive through the country.

"Ya won't. She sleeps like a vampire living in Svalbard, Norway," Bruce gave a mischievous grin and chuckled at his own joke before saying louder, "Don't ya, Maura?"

Elodie glanced back, but Maura didn't move or answer.

She turned her attention back to Bruce. "I have to ask."

"Ask."

She adjusted in her seat, turning slightly so she could watch him more easily. "A vampire living in Svalbard, Norway? Why is that funny?"

"Midnight sun," Bruce answered.

Elodie continued to stare at him.

"In Northern Europe, there is no sunset for half the year. Vampires have a natural aversion to sunlight because of the whole dying thing, so they sleep during the day. It's part of the Norwegian tourist package for supernaturals—the lack of nocturnal creatures during that time. In Northern Scotland, we had sustained twilight. The sun does set but not very far under the horizon." Bruce chuckled again. "Aye, that, and Maura married a dhampir."

Elodie realized how unprepared she was for the supernatural world. "Dhampir?"

"Descendant of a vampire and human," he explained. "Rare."

Elodie again looked at Maura sleeping.

"Does he…?"

"No. He is not a vampire," Bruce said. "No blood. No sun aversion. Though Jefferson does make a great mojito."

"There is so much I don't understand about

your world." She glanced at Bruce's. "So, if you were to have a baby with a human, what would it be called?"

"Loved," he answered as if it was the simplest question in the world.

Elodie couldn't help but smile. "No, seriously."

"MacGregor," he said.

"Half warlock, half human," she persisted.

"Warlock." He reached across the seat to take her hand. "Magick is inherited and taught. Vampirism is like a," he adjusted the rearview mirror to look at his sister before whispering, "contagion."

She felt her hand tingle and glanced down to see threads of blue weaving between them. The sensation drew up her arm to slow her heartbeat and settle her stomach. She took a deep, calming breath and relaxed.

"Can you teach me that?" she asked.

"What?"

"To summon magickal valium," she laughed, not knowing how else to explain it.

"Some magick can be taught, but anytime ya want it, it's yours." His hand tightened on hers. "Surely ya know by now, lassie. Everything I am is yours."

He dropped her hand to touch her cheek. His

eyes strayed from the road as if he didn't really need to pay attention to the driving.

"I love ya, Elodie."

Pleasure filled her, and her breath caught. Before Elodie could answer, Maura groaned.

"Uh, gross. Ya cannot propose to her in the car, Bruce," Maura scolded sleepily. She turned in the seat so that her back faced the front. "Elodie, don't put up with that. Ya deserve better."

"I'm not proposing in the car," Bruce denied.

"Sounded like ya were," Maura countered.

"I'm definitely not proposing with my annoying sister in the backseat," he argued.

"I think ya were."

"I think you're stupid."

Maura laughed. "Touché."

Elodie watched them in amusement.

"Do ya have siblings, Elodie?" Maura asked.

"No. It's just me," she answered.

"Lucky." Maura didn't turn back around.

"I have a couple of cousins—my dad's brother's sons. We're not close. I think they're in the south of France right now with their families."

"I wish I could send my cousins to the south of France." Maura suppressed a yawn. "Are we there yet?"

"Past Chicago. Crossing into Indiana." Bruce adjusted the rearview mirror back into place.

"Ya drive like a grandma," Maura muttered.

Elodie didn't say anything, as they were making unreal time. She watched cars maneuver out of their way to let them speed past.

"Do you think if I just canceled my phone service, that might break Jim's curse?" Elodie reasoned. "Or never used a phone again? People are addicted to their smartphones anyway. It might be good for me not to have one."

"I wish it was that easy. Not using the phone just blocked his delivery system. At best, we bought some time," Maura said. "If he's determined, he'll find another way to—"

"Maura," Bruce interrupted.

"I'm not going to lie to her." Maura twisted in the seat to meet Elodie's gaze. "We're going to do everything we can to stop this."

"I know." Elodie couldn't help feeling guilty. "Thank you. I will never be able to repay your family for what you're doing for me. I'm just so sorry that I brought this danger to you and your family."

"It's not your fault," Maura said.

"Ya didn't bring this to us." Bruce rested his hands on the steering wheel. "There is a reason ya were brought to Green Vallis. My magick must have sensed ya were in danger and called to ya to protect ya. MacGregor magick would not be part of the curse, but it has interrupted the curse. That is why everything became messed up with my artwork. When we petrified ya in the motel room with the intent of protecting ya, ya should have been protected and in a deep sleep. Instead, ya leaped into the television programs I was watching. Ya were trapped, but I could communicate with ya. Our magick sent ya someplace safe when the petrifying spell ended, so ya showed up at the house."

"And the drawings?"

"Raibeart and I had enchanted my paints so their murals couldn't be removed from the motel walls," Bruce said.

"They were doing it to annoy me," Maura put forth. "It worked. Try presenting Mr. and Mrs. Small Town Family with a room that has naked Medusa painted on the wall."

Bruce smirked. "Oh, come on. Not fully naked, and it's a story they'll be telling at parties for the rest of their lives."

"So they should thank ya?" Maura sat up and leaned forward between the front seats.

"Anyway," Bruce waved his hand in front of his sister's face to urge her to sit back, "I painted Echidna, a half-snake, half-woman."

"Yeah, we talked about this," Elodie said.

"*We* didn't," Maura prompted. "Keep going."

"I'm assuming that's when the curse merged with my magick," Bruce continued as if he hadn't been interrupted. "She came to life. I sent her back into her painting, but a smudge of a woman appeared next to her. Ya were bitten by a snake, but it wasn't fatal. Stopping Echidna interrupted the curse."

"As much as I hate to admit when ya are right, that explanation makes sense," Maura said.

"And this morning? The spiders in the motel room?" Elodie asked.

"He probably amplified his efforts," Maura said. "Think of it as curse and magick fighting over ya."

Having some answers was comforting, but not as much as she had thought it would be. She still didn't understand why.

"Magick is going to win," Bruce stated.

"How?" Elodie asked.

"I liked Uncle Raibeart's idea of dropping him headfirst into an active volcano." Maura yawned as she laid back down on the seat. She fluffed the pillow under her head and pulled the blanket up to block the sun from her face.

"I can get behind that plan," Bruce agreed.

Under normal circumstances, Elodie would never want to kill anyone. It went against her nature. Of course, she'd never been under magickal attack by her mother's employee before, either.

"Wake me up when there's food," Maura said. "Aunt Margareta packed nothing but boxes of raisins."

"Hand me a couple of those." Bruce reached his hand back.

"I ate them all." Maura laughed.

Elodie stared at the hypnotic pavement lines, watching the road come at them. Each second felt as if it carried a warning. How long would it take Jim to realize his texts weren't going through? How long before the curse dropped her out of an airplane or put her in the middle of a burning building?

Bruce took her hand and sent calming magick up her arm. As if reading her fears, he said, "I'm right here, love. No matter what happens, I'll be here for ya."

Chapter Nineteen

Elodie had driven into New York City many times, usually with a car service. Her eyes found familiar bridges, landscapes, and buildings. The current of people was never exactly the same, and yet it was. They moved over the sidewalks, ebbing and flowing like a swollen river, breaking off at corners.

The fast food burger they'd picked up in Pennsylvania along the way unsettled her stomach. In truth, anything would have. By the time they crossed into Manhattan, the knot building in her chest had become painful. She wanted to run.

She looked at the tall buildings engulfing the cars and felt like they might crumble over on top of them at any moment. She saw the manhole covers and expected a flood to come up and wash away the streets, taking them with it. Each passing car could have held a gunman. The danger was everywhere. The mounting fear tried to take over until she found it hard to stay calm.

What was Jim planning? Why? There is no way of knowing the answer to that question.

"Bruce, I—"

Elodie barely got the words out before the sounds of the street stopped, and her vision went black. She found herself sitting alone in the darkness. The car seat cushion turned into hard metal that pressed against her hips and lower back. The seatbelt had disappeared from her waist.

"Bruce?" she called out and startled surprise.

Panic surged through her. Tears threatened. She slowly lowered herself off the chair onto a dirty concrete floor. Bits of gravel and debris met her hands as she crawled, sweeping her fingers back and forth to get a sense of her surroundings. Water dripped steadily into a puddle, sounding far away. It was the only noise not created by her movements.

Elodie's hand frantically passed over a sharp object. She yelped in surprise at the painful sting. Blood poured from a cut on her finger. She felt it dripping down her hand and arm when she lifted it. Unsure what to do, she wrapped the wound with the edge of her t-shirt to soak up the blood.

"Hello?" she called. "Can anyone hear me?"

She wasn't sure making noise was the best idea. She could well guess this was not a safe place by the musty smell choking any freshness from the air, tainted with the hint of rot and unclean bodies.

"Jim, can you hear me? Why are you doing this to me? Please, can't we talk about this and work it out?" She begged. "Whatever it is, I'm sorry. I never meant to offend you or hurt you or insult you. Please, stop this!"

He didn't answer. She wasn't sure if that was comforting or not. If she heard a mocking laugh, she would know that she wasn't alone in this place. Then maybe she would have a chance to talk to him and explain and reason and beg.

"I'm not a bad person," she whispered. "Why are you doing this to me?"

The sound of dripping water was constant. Elodie kept her bleeding hand balled around the hem of her t-shirt. She pushed to her feet, sweeping her uninjured hand through the air. When she felt no surrounding walls, she reached above her. The back of her hand smacked into a hanging light bulb. She felt the light brush of the string as it began swinging back and forth. She fumbled around in the darkness to grab hold of it. Catching the string, she pulled it hard.

Dim yellow light flooded what looked to be a basement. The crumbling concrete floor was littered with dust and broken glass. She released the hem of her shirt to study the cut on her finger. It was deep and oozed, so she found a fresh spot of the shirt to rewrap it. She again held it against her stomach.

Elodie considered her surroundings. The chair she had been on was bolted to the floor. Used plastic ties were cut and left near the chair legs as if somebody had tied a person to it, only to release them later. Discoloration on the floor could have been many things that she did not want to imagine or think about. Who owned this place? And when would they be back?

"Jim, please," she whispered, trying to take a trembling breath and only managing several sharp gasps. "Please, please, please…"

Elodie did not expect the begging to work, but the words came out of her from fear until she realized she didn't only beg Jim but also whoever owned this room. Her mind tried to conjure up what type of person would need a place like this. What kind of things would they do? Who would they hold here? None of the answers brought her comfort.

She looked for a way out. If there was a way in, there had to be a way out. What she found was a door fitted in an alcove higher than the rest of the ceiling. At some point, stairs would have joined the basement to the first floor. But those were long gone. The cinder block walls did not create sound footing to climb up. Someone would need to lower a ladder. It was the perfect prison.

The dripping water came from a leaking pipe near a basement window. Elodie went to look out. Someone had painted the panes black from the outside, so she couldn't scrape them clean. She looked around for a weapon to break the glass. Since her hand was already bleeding, she didn't want to resort to punching it.

Was this place even real? She could be in the basement of some sicko's house for all she knew. Or she could be trapped in a mafia movie. How often had she watched true crime episodes from the safety of her bed? How many horror movies had she seen with this exact setup?

"...please, please, please..."

In no reality did a room like this include a friendly grandma holding a plate full of warm, delicious cookies.

"Calm down, Elodie. Bruce will find you. He won't stop looking until he finds you," she told herself. It was the only thought that brought her comfort. "And until that happens, you must try to find a way out. You are not helpless. Fuck Jim. Stop begging that asshole."

Elodie grabbed the chair and shook it violently, trying to break it free from the floor. She needed both hands, which only caused her finger to bleed more. She kicked at the legs where the concrete was crumbling. She managed to wiggle it back and forth. Rusted bolts pulled free, and she was slowly able to pry it up.

"Fuck you, Jim, you pansy ass coward," she swore under her breath.

She lifted the chair and shoved the leg at the window to break it. A leg busted through before hitting security bars. She put the chair on the ground and stepped up to look through the hole at an alleyway. A junkie lay several feet away with a needle sticking out of his arm.

"Hey!" she yelled. The man didn't budge. He was too far gone into his own problems.

Hearing a latch overhead, she pressed against the wall. Her hands gripped the back of the chair. The metal slide of a ladder came down from above, finding footing on the concrete floor. She held her breath as someone climbed down.

"Who left the light on?" a man grumbled. His distinctly New York accent told her she was probably still in the city. "What am I? Made of money?"

Elodie held her breath as feet ambled down the ladder. She made herself as small as possible against the wall. A beefy dude with too tight a shirt stepped past her bad hiding spot with a hand reaching out toward the light string. He paused and looked down, swearing under his breath at the missing chair.

Elodie swung the chair aiming for the back of his head. The man grunted and fell forward hard against the concrete floor. She released the chair and hurried for the ladder, scurrying up as fast as she could. The man in the basement yelled obscenities at her.

When she reached the top, she found the ladder too heavy to lift with her injured hand. She pushed the ladder over to buy herself time.

She found herself in a dilapidated house. The walls were crumbling, and the yellowed wallpaper was torn. The smell was much worse than the basement. Old mats were pressed up against the wall. Needles and trash had been kicked into every edge and corner they could fill. Squatters had painted profanities on the walls.

Elodie escaped out of the front door into a neighborhood that had seen better days. The drug addicts stumbling down the street were worse off than the zombies she had seen at the farm. This was a hell of human making, and she knew staying put for too long wasn't safe. The thug in the basement would find his way back up, and she did not know his intentions.

Elodie ran down the street, not knowing where she was going. If this were New York City, as she suspected, then she would find a landmark soon enough. She might not know where the MacGregor home was, but she could find her home. With any luck, Bruce would find her there.

She cradled her hand against her stomach and held on to her wrist. Hunching her shoulders, she ran, not wanting to draw attention to herself and hoping the bloodied shirt would be enough to keep strangers away. The great thing about the city was that people were trained to mind their own business. And if you saw a bloody mess running past you, you knew better than to stop and fuck with them.

Chapter Twenty

Elodie should have said I love you.

When Bruce said it in the car, she should have said it back regardless of his sister making jokes in the back seat. What if she never got another chance? She tried not to think like that, but it was difficult with an aching hand and a curse chasing her.

She felt that at any second, she might disappear from the subway car and end up buried alive in an unmarked grave or thrown in the back of a van or held up at knifepoint by one of her traveling companions. Her mind had no problem conjuring frightening scenarios. And those weren't even the supernatural ones. The possibilities were as vast as Jim's sick imagination: haunted houses, portals to Hell, demon possession, gremlins, goblins, the Abominable Snowman, and alien abductions. Who knew what the man would think of next?

Thankfully, some slick-haired executive had given her five dollars to get away from him, which she used for the subway fare. Otherwise, it would have been a long trek home. Elodie exited the subway and began running toward her parents' building.

In the borough of Manhattan near the neighborhood where her parents lived, a bloody outfit wouldn't go as unnoticed. She tucked the stained material of her long sleeve t-shirt into her blue jeans to hide the evidence.

Brushing her fingers through her hair in hopes of straightening it, she adjusted her posture and strode toward the doorman of the building.

"Good evening, Miss Elodie." Harris had been the doorman for over a decade, ever since moving up north from Mississippi. He always had a smile for her. "I didn't know you were back in town."

"Hey, Mr. Harris. I just got back." She smiled, cradling her hand. "How's the family?"

"Doin' good. Thank you." He held open the door. His eyes dropped to her hands. "You're bleeding, Miss Elodie."

"Yeah, some idiot left a broken bottle on the subway." She gave a nervous dismissive laugh.

"I'm going to see if my mother has a first aid kit in the house and get it cleaned up."

"We have one in the employee lounge. Come with me, and we'll get it fixed in a jiffy." Harris did not look like he was about to take no for an answer. He gestured for her to follow him.

Elodie walked with him behind the security desk into the small employee lounge. Within minutes Harris had her wound cleaned out and superglued it shut before wrapping a bandage around it.

"The guys in maintenance are cutting themselves all the time," he said. "This should fix it right up. Would you like some aspirin for the pain?"

"No, thank you," Elodie answered. "Thank you for this. Can you tell me if my mother is home?"

"Far as I know," Harris said. "Your father is in California and isn't expected back for another week."

She already knew that.

"Is anyone with her?" Elodie asked.

Harris suppressed a small smile. He looked at the door to the employee lounge before lowering his voice and leaning into her. "Just that little troll doll that follows her around all the time. You know the one." He lifted his hand above his head and gestured upward. "The rude one with the hair."

The man had an infectious laugh.

Elodie smiled and stood. "I always loved your honesty, Harris."

"You're about the only one in this building who does," he answered. "So, can I count you in for a game tonight? That Lewis in maintenance has a wad of singles burning a hole in his pocket that I think we can take off him. Poor kid doesn't have a poker face to save his life."

"Oh, sorry, not tonight." Elodie went to the door to leave. She held up her hand and said, "Thanks for this, doctor."

"Anytime, little lady, anytime."

They parted ways. Harris returned to his post at the door, and Elodie made her way to the elevators. She passed a few of the building's residents coming out as she stepped inside the elevator. For a moment, she hesitated and thought about telling Harris to expect Bruce and Maura. But, in the end, she decided they would probably have a magickal way up.

Her hand shook as she punched in the security code for the penthouse. She wasn't sure what she would do when she saw Jim. In fact, every part of her wanted to send the elevator right back down to the lobby so she could run away. But there was nowhere to run. The curse would find her, and it would have a brand new creative hell for her to survive.

She had no choice.

She had to do this.

Elodie watched the lights move up the panel as the elevator ascended. Her hand lifted a couple of times, and she had to stop herself from pushing other buttons to slow the ride. The lights flickered, and she grabbed hold of the safety rail and held on tight. She thought of the elevator dropping, of the cables snapping and sending her into freefall.

Elodie was tired of being afraid. She was tired of her mind imagining horrible things. She wanted to be back in Wisconsin with Bruce in the motel. She knew what she wanted. She wanted that life with him. Despite Maura's teasing, he had not asked her to marry him, but she'd say yes if he did. She wanted to say yes. She loved him, and for the first time in her life, she knew exactly what she wanted. She wanted a life with Bruce.

A perfect, simple life with Bruce.

That one dream gave her strength, and she stared at the lights on the panel, counting down until she reached the top of the building. When the doors finally opened, she peeked out into the foyer of the home. It was empty. A painting and two decorative vases grazed the small area beside the front door. She punched the door code into the security panel to unlock it before entering.

Elodie opened the door slowly. It didn't make a noise. She poked her head inside first, getting a sense of the area. Soft jazz music played on a record player. She never knew whether her mother really liked jazz or thought it was cool to enjoy jazz. Her mother seemed to make many decisions based on what she thought other people would think of her and her family rather than what she wanted for herself. It was a very sad existence.

Normally Elodie would call out to announce her presence. Instead, she moved deliberately through the home, searching for who was there. By this time of the day, the maids would be gone. Since Janelle was always on a diet, the cook would have prepared a salad which she would have left in the fridge. The house was only fully staffed in the evening if there was a party or a photo shoot.

Floor to ceiling windows presented a balcony that overlooked the city below. A glass railing encased it to prevent people from going over. Elodie crossed to the window to look outside. Cushioned chairs were anchored to the ground to keep them from blowing away. A shiver worked over her as she remembered the last bolted chair she had seen in the city basement.

Her family had lived in this building since she was a child, at least whenever they were in the city. Standing there, seeing what had to be the fifteenth complete redecoration in her lifetime, none of it felt like home. She could not think of a single house her parents owned that felt like a home. Everything was beautiful, rich, and perfectly placed. She remembered wishing the walls would cave in on her as a child.

The penthouse seemed a strange contrast to the MacGregor mansion. Yes, Bruce's family was just as wealthy, if not more so, and they were surrounded by very fine things. But the air felt differently when the family sat at the table together. Even when they were bickering and poking at each other, it felt unmistakable. There was an energy in the air, an indescribable feeling that connected them. And she had the distinct impression that they would die for each other without question, without having to be asked. For all their pranks and jokes and teasing, there was love in the MacGregor family.

Elodie wanted to be a part of that. She desperately wanted that in her life. She wanted it with Bruce.

The certainty of her thoughts gave her strength. She turned away from the balcony to look over the living room. Fresh cut flowers filled several vases. No light came from the direction of the kitchen, so she headed toward the master suite. As she walked past a bookcase, she grabbed a solid statuette of a fairy creature and held it like a weapon. The bronze figure would not break upon impact.

Elodie tried to keep her steps soft on the carpet. Between each one, she paused, calculating changes in her surroundings. Dim overhead night-lights were on a timer. She slowed as she passed by the bathroom door. She followed the sound of music only to stop when it paused. She waited until a new song began before continuing forward.

Her mother's bedroom door was cracked open, and she saw the light coming from within. Elodie leaned to peek inside. Beneath the music, she heard the murmur of soft voices.

"That's it. Drink up, beautiful." Jim was with her mother.

"Are you sure this is working? It tastes horrible." Her mother's words were slurred as if she had spent the evening drinking. That would not be anything new for the esteemed Mrs. Fairweather. Sobriety had never been a priority.

"That's how you know it's working," Jim supplied. "You, of all people, know that beauty is pain and sacrifice. Now be a good girl and finish your magick tonic. You want to be ready for the cameras, don't you?"

Magick tonic? Elodie frowned. Did her mother know about magick?

"Is my daughter coming?" Her mother's voice had softened into a sleepy murmur. "They won't do it if she's not here. She said this is a societal piece about mothers who look like their daughter…sister…daughter."

"Yes, I told her how important this was to you." Jim's voice had a pout to it. "She doesn't care. She says she's not coming home. I've told you she is ungrateful and doesn't deserve you."

"Don't say that. My daughter loves me," her mother mumbled in protest.

"Say it," Jim ordered.

"My daughter is ungrateful and doesn't deserve me," Janelle repeated.

"That's right," Jim said. "That's a good girl. Now tell me, who does deserve you?"

"You." The word was barely audible, as if her mother was already asleep when she mumbled it.

"That's right," Jim agreed. "And what idea are you going to have tomorrow?"

"Lawyer."

"That's right."

Elodie felt her eye twitch.

Asshole.

A strange red glow came from within the bedroom, flickering like bad neon.

Elodie gripped the statue tighter. She wasn't sure how to handle this. Did she barge into the room and confront him or hide in the corner like she had in the basement and hit him from behind when he stepped through the doorway? She pressed her back against the wall and held the bronze fairy up, ready to strike.

"I know you're there, princess," Jim stated. "Come in if you're coming in."

Chapter Twenty-One

Bruce looked into the face that mirrored his own, not needing to say a word. He and Rory had always had a connection, though they were not mental carbon copies of each other. Whereas Bruce often forgot about things like haircuts and designer clothes, his twin embraced such things. Rory's styled brown hair was tipped with blond. His tailored silk shirt was a souvenir from his recent trip to Italy with his new wife, Jennifer.

Walking with them down the sidewalk was Maura. She hadn't said much since Elodie disappeared from the car mid-sentence. They had been confident there would be more time to confront Jim, but the fact that the man was able to regroup and continue his curse so quickly revealed just how powerful of an enemy they faced.

"Do ya know what kind of creature we're dealing with?" Rory asked.

"Elodie thought he was a human." Maura walked faster. She tucked her hands into her front pockets. Her pace prompted them to speed up next to her.

"From what you're telling me, this Jim does not sound like a human. And if he is, he had to have made a deal with the devil to draw upon this much power." Rory pulled on Maura and Bruce's arms, slowing them as they neared Elodie's building.

"Or wizard," Bruce said, his throat constricting. "Or witch. Or—"

"We get it," Rory put forth. Though he had been traveling for days, his brother's eyes looked alert. They had told him everything that had happened and the short walk over from the MacGregor Manhattan house. "Did ya try drawing her to communicate with her to find out where she's at?"

"Aye." Bruce tried to speed up, and Rory again pulled him back to slow his pace. "I've tried everything I can think of to get Elodie back, but we have no clue where to look. That is what's so frustrating about this curse. We never know how it's going to manifest. She could be anywhere on this world or in a fantasy realm. She could be trapped in a television commercial or inside a book. He could have her inside a painting or somebody's attic in Kansas locked in a trunk. There is no pattern to his attacks."

"It's whatever random thing he comes up with at the time, and there's no predicting what that will be," Maura added.

"I don't have to point out that if we stop him, that doesn't necessarily mean we will stop the curse." Rory's tone was annoyingly reasonable. "I know you're angry, Bruce, but ya want to keep a level head. Let's find out what's going on first, and then ya can kill the bloody bastard."

"Oh, aye," Bruce swore, his hand balling into a fist, ready to make contact.

Suddenly, Rory stopped walking and pulled them to stop with him. Bruce looked at him in question, and a simple hand gesture told Bruce everything he needed to know.

Rory strode up to the doorman with a big smile and easily struck up a conversation about baseball and world champion poker tournaments. The sound of their enthusiastic voices carried over to them. Maura and Bruce naturally turned toward each other like they were having their own conversation.

Bruce's magick surged inside of him in anticipation. It drew from Central Park, and as much as he loved nature, he knew he'd destroy every plant in the city if that meant saving Elodie.

Within seconds Rory was waving his hand behind him, urging his siblings to sneak inside. The doorman kept chatting as if he couldn't see the two people sneaking past him. Bruce and Maura went to the elevators. When they looked toward the front door, their brother was waving goodbye to the doorman as he came to join them.

"The Fairweathers own the penthouse," Rory said as if he'd garnished that information from his chat.

"I know. Elodie told me," Bruce went inside the elevator and waved his hand over the security keypad. The door shut, and the elevator took them upward.

"Thank ya for coming back, Rory," Bruce said. "And thank ya, Maura, for being here. I can't tell ya how much this means to me."

"Ya don't even have to say it, brother," Maura answered.

"She better be ok," Bruce whispered to himself. Magick swirled over his clenched fists. He felt it tingling inside of him, ready to explode. "She better be ok."

Rory put his hand on Bruce's shoulder, trying

to calm him. "She will be. Your magick called to her in Wisconsin. It's protecting her even now. Have faith."

The doors opened on the penthouse level, and Bruce didn't hesitate as he waved his hand at the security panel to force the front door open.

He felt his magick building, moving from his fist up his arms. It wrapped around his neck, almost choking him with the heat of its intensity. He heard Rory and Maura moving behind him. His sister turned to the right, and Rory went across the living room to a balcony.

"Show yourself," Bruce ordered, watching for the yellow markers that would tell him where everybody was located in the house. Seeing indicator lights coming through a door at the end of a long hallway, Bruce didn't wait for his siblings as he turned to follow them.

The sound of music came from inside the room. The static underlying the song sounded like it came from an old record player. He didn't recognize the jazz artist, but the melody was sad. He reached out with his magick lifting his hands to point the palms forward as he readied himself for battle.

Bruce heard his siblings rushing behind him. He didn't wait.

Bruce shoved open the door and barged

inside. He raised his hand, ready to fire. Seconds before he released his power, Elodie's eyes met his, and he managed to stop the attack. They were wide with fear and swimming with red. Her body levitated off the floor, and Bruce didn't know if she could see him. Her jaw hung slack as if she had no control over it. Her entire body shook violently, like a rag doll being beaten by an invisible, angry child.

"Elodie!" Bruce yelled.

She didn't answer him.

The door slammed shut behind him. It stopped Maura and Rory from entering the room. Fists pounded on the door, and he could hear the sizzle of magick as they threw everything they had to try to get inside with him.

"Show yourself," Bruce ordered. Yellow sparkling lights lifted from the bed and from Elodie but nowhere else.

A woman slept on the bed. She moaned softly but didn't wake up. The yellow lights revealed enough of her face for Bruce to conclude it was Elodie's mother. They had the same beautiful features, only Janelle looked as if she'd had the help of a plastic surgeon.

Bruce stepped closer to Elodie, trying to keep an eye on her while also searching the room for her attacker. "Who are ya? Show yourself, Jim. Or Roberto. Whatever ya call yourself, coward!"

Maura was right. They were not dealing with a human. No human he had ever known in all his years could create this type of dark magick.

"Bruce! Open the door," Rory ordered as the fists continued to pound.

At the same time, Maura yelled, "Bruce, can ya hear us? Let us in!"

"Jim," Bruce stated, not trying to keep the anger out of his tone. "I guarantee ya do not want to make enemies of the warlocks MacGregor. Even if ya beat us here tonight, the others will come for ya. They know what you've been up to. And we're not happy."

A strange clicking and tapping noise answered Bruce's threat. Bruce spun around to face a figure standing in the shadows near the head of Janelle's bed.

Jim didn't look like a man. The hunched, disfigured form jerked forward with a stilted step. No, this was an older creature from a time before the birth of the first vampires. And vampires were fucking old as dirt.

"Incubus," Bruce whispered in realization. The word literally meant a nightmare induced by a demon. It was said that the incubus started as a collection of thoughts so dark and deadly that they manifested into something that could not be killed. Over time it had become ravenous and greedy. It was the complete sum of everything wrong and bad in humanity.

Jim clicked and gurgled. The grotesque sound was almost like laughter. A creature this old would not be scared of a warlock clan. Bruce doubted he would fear anything.

"Ya can't have her." Bruce kept his magick at the ready. He pointed his finger toward the door blasting magick toward it to destroy the wooden barrier. With his siblings pushing at the other side, they all managed to splinter it open.

Rory came in, arm raised with magick, ready to blast anyone in his path. "What the…?"

"Incubus," Bruce said.

Maura was more cautious as she surveyed what was happening. Seeing Elodie, she rushed to her side. Elodie hovered in her trap, convulsing and moaning.

"Weren't they all put to sleep like centuries ago?" Rory asked.

"Apparently, this one woke up," Bruce quipped.

"Do ya smell that?" Maura couldn't get Elodie down, so she stood in front of her like a shield. She swept her hand toward the record player, causing the needle to scratch across the vinyl. The music stopped. "I know my potions. That's possession tea."

Bones snapped as Jim's form contorted and jerked.

"Fuck this," Rory swore. He threw a magick ball at the incubus. The creature easily avoided it and continued his clicking and laughing. His eyes glowed red, the color matching Elodie's gaze.

"Something's not right here," Maura stated.

"No shit, dumbass," Rory answered. "What gave ya the first clue? Mr. Ugly over there?"

"No, smartass," Maura asserted. "An incubus would not need to use possession tea on anyone. And he sure as hell wouldn't have any need to cast a curse. If he wanted to harm this family, he would do it. He wouldn't need to send text messages to make somebody fall into a nightmare. Jim can't be one of the ancients."

"Then what the hell is he?" Bruce demanded. "Because I know what I'm looking at."

"Half incubus, half human," Maura deduced. "I'm guessing all the ugly, half the power."

Jim's bones snapped again. This time, they kept snapping, popping with loud horrible punctuations of sound. Narrowed hands shifted and formed into what looked like human fingers. Jim stepped out of the shadows as his skin smoothed and his figure reformed.

"This family is mine," Jim stated. His eyes still glowed with red as if feeding off Elodie. "Get your own free ride, warlocks."

Jim said *warlocks* with such disgust as if the word tasted terrible just passing over his lips.

"This family is under MacGregor protection," Bruce said.

Jim suddenly roared. Red magick burst out of him in a fiery rage. It scorched the bedding and melted the carpet at his feet. It flung the warlocks back.

Bruce's arms flailed as he was lifted off the ground under the force of a powerful tidal wave of magick. Rory cried out as he was shoved out the broken door and down the hallway. The sound of glass and wood crashing followed him. Maura was flipped over, knocking upside down and face first into the wall. The impact was so great that the impression of her body held her in place for a few seconds before she fell to the ground, unmoving.

Bruce pushed to his feet. His magick had taken a blow and had dissipated. Never in his life had he been hit with something so strong. He smelled the singed material of his plaid kilt. His calves and forearms felt as if he had walked through fire. Blisters bubbled over his hands.

He didn't stop to think. The fire that hit him

had carried with it a rage that lingered. He began yelling, throwing everything he had at Jim. He charged forward, hands outstretched as he reached for the man's neck. He felt Jim's throat beneath his fingers and squeezed as hard as he could. His knees lifted, aiming for any piece of the creature he could reach.

A soft cry came from Elodie's direction. He heard a thump as she landed on the floor.

"Bruce," her weak voice groaned. "Bruce."

The sound only made him fight harder. He struggled to pin Jim to the floor. Maura crawled toward him to help. Jim blasted them again with red rage, this time singeing Bruce's hair. He smelled it burning and kept fighting.

Maura threw weak magick as she fought to stay conscious. Rory stumbled in, swaying as he fell more than leaped into the fray. Maura finally managed to reach them as she rolled herself into the fight.

Jim's spine cracked beneath his fingers, but Bruce refused to let go. Jim bucked and thrashed, screeching in anger.

Suddenly, Elodie joined the fight. She flung herself down onto what had become a magickal dog pile. They all rolled. Fists flew. Fingers gouged. Nails clawed. He even felt teeth briefly anchor into his arm.

Elodie screamed as she was flung back. Bruce roared with anger to see her from the corner of his eye. His body pulled energy, killing all the cut flowers in the house before pulling from outside. He shoved everything he had into his hands. Blue burst out of him.

Jim jerked off the floor to levitate with Bruce on top of him before collapsing lifeless.

They landed hard, the force jarring them apart. Bruce fell onto the rough texture of melted carpet fibers. He kicked his foot to the side to strike Jim one last time. Dead eyes stared back.

Bruce grunted as he crawled in the direction Elodie had flown. Maura gave a weak moan as she lay on her stomach. Bruce passed his sister, reaching to lightly touch her before moving on.

Elodie lay motionless on the opposite side of the bed. Patchy red splotches covered her face and neck. He instantly reached for her and felt her pulse beating against his fingers. Her chest rose and fell with breath. She was alive. For the moment, that's all that mattered.

"Rory?" Bruce called out hoarsely.

Rory groaned. "Need a minute, brother. Maura?"

"*Uhh*," was all their sister said.

"Someone check Elodie's mother," Bruce ordered.

It took a moment, but Rory crawled to the edge of the bed and lifted himself up to check on the woman.

"Alive," Rory said as he collapsed forward on the mattress. His knees were still on the floor as he half lay on the bed. "Asleep."

"Elodie?" Maura asked.

"I have her," Bruce said, only to whisper toward Elodie, "I have ya, love. I have ya."

"Jim?" Maura asked.

"Dead," Bruce answered.

"Good," Maura grumbled. "Ow, the fucking prick."

No one was in a hurry to move. Bruce kept Elodie next to him. He wished he had enough magick to calm her, even as she was unconscious. But the battle had fried his energy, and it had to be enough that they were both breathing.

Elodie moaned.

"You're safe," Bruce put forth before she could say anything. "It's over. Jim's dead."

She moaned again.

"Your ma is safe. Rory and Maura too. Everything is going to be all right," Bruce promised. "It's over."

"Nice to meet ya, Elodie," Rory muttered, not moving from his position on the bed.

Elodie's eyes rolled as if she had trouble focusing on his face.

"Stay with me, love," Bruce insisted.

Her lips moved, and it looked like she mouthed the word, "Forever," before her lashes fluttered and her eyes closed.

Chapter Twenty-Two

Elodie imagined this was what it felt like to recover from a car accident if that car had been driven off the side of a cliff and then rolled over with a steamroller while being buried under an avalanche. Everything ached, from the roots of her hair to her nail beds to her ribs every time she tried to move. Her skin felt bruised, and her nerves felt raw.

Luckily, she did not look as bad as she felt to the outside world. None of them did. Rory had cast something called a glamour spell to hide the fact that their hair had been nearly singed off and their skin looked like they were extras in a post-apocalyptic fire world.

Janelle Fairweather had not been pleased to find her room a wreck. By the time she woke up from the potion Jim had given her, they had managed to hide the half incubus's body. Elodie did not ask what they did with it, but she did hear Maura say something about hallowed ground and a friendly local church that would look the other way.

Elodie told her mother they had caught Jim stealing from her when they arrived. And in an effort to get away, he had started a fire. Janelle was only too willing to file that police report, turning the story into her firsthand account of survival and betrayal so that she would be the one to be interviewed by reporters when the story broke. And Janelle made sure the story broke. Her mother would dine out on that trauma for years.

"Ready?" Bruce held out his hand to her.

They stood on the tarmac as the MacGregor jet came to a stop in the distance to pick them up. Bruce's twin, Rory, acted nothing like him. He was with his wife, Jennifer. She seemed sweet, if not a little upset about being left behind during the family's latest battle. Maura stood holding a phone, video calling with her husband. Elodie could hear her reassuring the man that she was unharmed.

"Ma said she would have a car waiting for us when we land in Wisconsin," Rory called over the sound of the engines. "We should be there in a few hours. She'll have healing potions waiting."

"What about Euann's car?" Elodie asked Bruce. "Doesn't someone need to drive it back?"

Rory heard the question and chuckled. "He can pick it up if he wants it." He laughed harder. "If he can find it."

"What do you mean? What happened to it?" Elodie inquired.

Rory grinned. "Just a little game of hide and seek. Trust me. My cousin has it coming."

"Come on. Let's go home," Jennifer pulled Rory toward the jet.

Bruce didn't move to follow them. "How are ya feeling?"

It was hardly the first time Bruce had asked her that question. Elodie could see the concern on his face every time he looked at her. The glamour spell had hidden their injuries from her view, but she wondered what they saw when they looked at her. The way Bruce searched her face and gingerly touched her anytime she was near made her think that he could see what was really there.

"I'll be fine," she told him. "We're all safe, and the curse is over. That's all that matters. I, for one, am happy not to worry about flipping through channels or being attacked by spiders."

Bruce slowly walked with her toward the jet.

She held back with him as the others loaded first. When they were relatively alone, she said, "I need to talk to you."

"What is it?"

"I should have said this in the car. I shouldn't have let Maura being there stop me. But I need to tell you something. It's important."

"What?" His expression filled with concern.

"I love you too. I hated myself for not saying it back. It was all I could think about when I was taken from the car. I love you too, Bruce. I love you so much. And I want to marry you. I don't want to waste time. I know you said you weren't asking, and your sister was there making jokes, but I guess I'm asking. Or telling. Or asking. Just…"

"Aye, my love. Let's get married. I love ya forever." He gently touched her cheek, careful not to hurt her. His lips slowly lowered to meet hers in a soft kiss. "Whatever ya want, it's yours."

"I want to be with you. I want to live at Hotel Motel, not in the mansion. I want you to teach me the motel business so I can be useful to you and your sister and not freeload. I want to write. Books, hopefully. I'm unsure if I will be good at it, but I want to try. I want you to do your artwork or whatever else brings you joy."

"Ya have given this some thought." Bruce grinned. "Is that all?"

Elodie shook her head. "No. I also want to be with you for however long I have on this earth."

Bruce grinned. "That's going to be a long time. Ya know, once we marry, my magick gets shared with ya. I hope ya still feel that way when you're four hundred years old."

Elodie's mouth opened in surprise. Four hundred?

"Hey, are ya coming or what?" Rory yelled. "Pilot is on a schedule. Don't make us leave ya behind."

"Aye, we're coming!" Bruce placed his hand on her lower back and guided her toward the stairs for boarding.

Elodie couldn't help but feel excitement as she stepped up into her future. So many emotions filled her. They were almost over-whelming.

"I'd like to present the future Mrs. Bruce MacGregor!" Bruce announced as they entered the cabin to find seats. Cheers erupted. He pointed at Rory. "Call Ma back and tell her to have the marriage book ready. We're not waiting a second longer than we have to."

"Ugh, Bruce," Maura groaned. "Tell me ya did not propose to her on the tarmac. Elodie deserves better than that."

"Actually, she proposed to me," Bruce

answered proudly. "So, meh!" He stuck his tongue out at her.

"Classy," Maura grumbled, leaning her seat back and closing her eyes. "Elodie, it's not too late to change your mind. Just say the word, and we can parachute to freedom."

"Nah." Elodie sat next to Bruce and held his hand. "I think I'm good."

"I know I'm good." Bruce took her hand and brought it to his lips. He placed soft kisses on her wrist. "I love ya, Elodie. Forever."

She took a deep breath and closed her eyes, no longer afraid of what might happen in the next second. "Let's go home."

The End

Warlocks MacGregor® Series

SCOTTISH MAGICKAL WARLOCKS

Love Potions
Spellbound
Stirring Up Trouble
Cauldrons and Confessions
Spirits and Spells
Kisses and Curses
Magick and Mischief
A Dash of Destiny
Night Magick
A Streak of Lightning
Magickal Trouble

Visit www.MichellePillow.com for details.

About Michelle M. Pillow

New York Times & *USA TODAY*
Bestselling Author

Michelle loves to travel and try new things, whether it's a paranormal investigation of an old Vaudeville Theatre or climbing Mayan temples in Belize. She believes life is an adventure fueled by copious amounts of coffee.

Newly relocated to the American South, Michelle is involved in various film and documentary projects with her talented director husband. She is mom to a fantastic artist. And she's managed by a dog and cat who make sure she's meeting her deadlines.

For the most part she can be found wearing pajama pants and working in her office. There may or may not be dancing. It's all part of the creative process.

**Come say hello! Michelle loves talking
with readers on social media!**

www.MichellePillow.com

facebook.com/AuthorMichellePillow

twitter.com/michellepillow

instagram.com/michellempillow

bookbub.com/authors/michelle-m-pillow

goodreads.com/Michelle_Pillow

amazon.com/author/michellepillow

youtube.com/michellepillow

pinterest.com/michellepillow

Please Leave a Review

THANK YOU FOR READING!

Please take a moment to share your thoughts by reviewing this book.

Be sure to check out Michelle's other titles at www.MichellePillow.com

Made in the USA
Thornton, CO
08/09/23 12:09:34